BIG DADDY

HEARTBREAKERS MC #4

ALEXIS ABBOTT

PATHFORGERS PUBLISHING

Get an EXCLUSIVE book, **FREE** just as a thank you for signing up for my newsletter! Plus you'll never miss a new release, cover reveal, or promotion!

http://alexisabbott.com/newsletter

BIG DADDY

Thundering engines roar across the dusty highway across the Great Plains, the sun blazing down on me as the two scouts I'm hunting down try to weave around me. The two kuttes in front of me aren't mine, and that's a problem. They belong to our rivals, and I caught them riding in our territory. I don't have time to wait for Tank, I'm going after them now and hoping he got my message, because I'm not letting them escape.

These runts have no place in Heartbreaker country. We're at war with the Buzzsaws, and the gloves are off. No excuses, no prisoners.

A bullet ricochets off the road way too close to me, and I veer to the side with a metal baseball bat held tightly in my hand before I tap the brakes and let the one behind me get close. Before he can steer away, I bring the bat backward, whipping it through the air so hard it sounds like a blade cutting it, and I hear a painful crack as it bounces off the biker's thigh.

He howls in pain and falls behind as I gun the acceleration. The guy riding ahead of me with his pistol out tries to pull back to fall in with me and line up a shot, but I'm way ahead of him. I swerve across him as he cuts through my lane, and I tap his muffler with my bat, letting out a grim chuckle as the dry wind whips around us. It's dangerous, of course. My life is dangerous. But it's also a thrill.

The black storm clouds in the distant plains behind us crackle with lightning, but the clear skies over us so far away make the bright browns and yellows around the cracked asphalt feel surreal. But my weapon's metal is every bit as real as the muscle backing it up, and I don't hold back. These fucking human traffickers are scum, and I'll root every last one of them out of Wyoming myself if that's what it takes.

Fine enforcer I'd be if I did anything less.

I lean the bike to the right and take a swing at the gunman, who fires into the air, missing wildly as he tries to avoid me. He curses up a storm as I stay close to him and only have to tear away when his buddy tries to come up on me from behind.

I use my bat like a spear to push the gunman, who nearly falls out of his seat before recovering and driving along the edge of the road while his comrade roars up to my left.

As he does, I notice his arm out in the rear-view mirror, and I see the black switchblade. I gun the acceleration and hurdle forward before the sharp blade can narrowly miss my kidney. My gloved knuckles are tight on the handles of my ride as the tons of screaming metal and gasoline charge ahead. As I go, I don't just swing the bat at the gunman, I fling it at him like a spear while I pass him.

It catches him at the elbow, and I hear a painful crack before his gun falls from the hand, firing into the asphalt as it hits the ground. That one's wounded, and I know he's the one I've got to go in for hard.

I veer to the left side of the road, riding parallel to the two, and with a hand like lightning, I take out the revolver at my side. Immediately, the unharmed man between us falls back, and I take aim at the other guy's tires.

With one shot, the biker yelps as his front tire bursts, and the rubber rips off the wheel in shreds as the motorcycle spins out. The biker is surprisingly good at keeping it from tumbling over and snapping him in half, but he careens off the side of the road into the dry grass near a warped, lightning-struck tree.

While his buddy is watching that unfold, I don't waste time--I bring my bike right on over to him and bring my elbow right into his jaw in time for him to turn to face me. His bike leans hard, and unlike his friend, it lays down as it runs into the dirt, and he manages to push himself from the bike before the two tumble separately in a cloud of dust.

My bike comes to a halt as soon as I can brake and wheel it back around, and I'm out of the seat in an instant. The man who laid the bike down is on his back, jaw slack and eyes closed. But I can see his chest rising and falling steadily, and a kick to his side confirms that he's out cold.

I approach the other man, the one with the injured limbs, who is on his stomach, limbs spread at awkward angles. As I approach, his right arm flexes, and I see it grip the knife in his hand--and my boot comes down on his wrist, hard.

"Fuck!" he cries as I hold my revolver trained on him.

"Don't," I grunt.

Ten minutes later, I have the two scouts tied together to the tree on their asses. The conscious one stares up at me sullenly, wincing in pain from his injuries as he watches me empty a can of kerosene on the two kuttes I yanked off them and tossed in a pile between us.

"You boys are a long way from home," I remark, squirting the last of the kerosene out and taking my time to toss it back in my bike's storage. "Think you'd get away riding with those colors around here? What the fuck were you doing?"

The scout just stares up at me with a scowl. He's young, probably just a prospect, but maybe not so young that he's innocent. I won't kill him unless he makes me, but he doesn't need to know that. After a few moments of silence, my stony gaze leaves him to drift down to the matches I take out of my pocket.

I strike one and toss it onto the kuttes, where the flame quickly blossoms over the kerosene and dry grass I gathered under it. The fire starts burning steadily, not really catching on the kuttes so much as burning the patches and slowly warping and cracking the leather and filling the air with the smell of burning hair. I stare him down over the flames while I cross my arms.

"See these?" I grunt, pointing down to the burning Buzzsaw kuttes. "These are you. If you're smart, you'll let this part of your lives burn out here and tell me what I want to know. And if you don't want to do that," I add, picking up my metal bat off the ground and giving it a casual twirl before planting it in the ground between my feet. "Then I'll show you how we handle Buzzsaws that get lost."

I could have sworn the scout pissed himself as his face paled.

"Orders came from Diesel through Chainlink-- his vice," the scout blurts, almost tripping over his words to start singing for me.

"I know who Chainlink is," I growl. "What are your orders?"

"Diesel wants to figure out your numbers on this side of the plains," he says through gritted teeth as he squirms, clearly pained by one of his several baseball bat injuries. "We know you're not making headway out west, so I assumed he wants to make a push down here."

"How many more scouts like you are there out here?" I ask, the pillar of my bat still unmoving.

"Just us," he swears, eyes wide and terrified. "Chainlink told us so. He doesn't want many men on the road, I guess he's trying to keep it quiet."

That all checks out, in my books.

The Heartbreakers MC got a formal declaration of war from Diesel's Buzzsaws, the MC he reformed around a human trafficking ring that's been forcing women into prostitution all over the state. Hell, the Heartbreakers were formed by our prez rescuing the first girl the Buzzsaws tried to get their hands on, and we've clashed with them at every turn ever since.

But the last skirmish we had outside an old mine was a bridge too far, and both sides are gearing up for war.

"Well aren't you helpful," I growl with an ominous smile as I pace around the fire, letting the metal bat drag noisily over the rocky ground. "Tell me more. We had reports of gunshots in Pine Haven, was that you too?"

"Not us, personally!" he stammered in a hurry. "Yeah, that was one of our prospects. They had him just fire off rounds, they want to piss the town off."

Fuck, I knew it. They're trying to turn the town and the mayor against us. We've had trouble with the mayor ever since Bones got into a fight with some fuckhead would-be date rapist who turned out to be a senator's son.

"Thought you might have had something to do with that," I growl, narrowing my eyes. "No blood, huh? Had a prospect's house on the border of your territory get shot up. His brother was there. He took a bullet. Those were civilians."

I kneel down next to the man and glare at him in the eye. "You don't even deny it."

"I didn't have anything to do with it," he swears, and I roll my eyes. "I-I don't know the names of who was involved in that!"

Before I can reply, I hear the sound of an engine roaring up behind me. I stand up slowly, bat still in hand and my other hand on my revolver. But it's a friendly face I see through the blurred light on the asphalt ahead.

Tank, the turncoat who joined us when he got wise to the sex trafficking operation, rumbles toward me on his bike and brings it to a slow stop with a broad grin on his face at my handiwork, surveying the scene.

"Well fuck me," he says as he hops off his bike and dusts his hands off, standing out of earshot of the prisoners on the side of the road but chuckling over at them. "Looks like you got a handle on things, alright."

"Wasn't joking," I said matter-of-factly. "See anyone else on the road? These two spies say they're the only ones in this neck of the woods, but they might have lied."

"Nothin'," Tank says. "Well, nothing but one scary motherfucker hanging out on the side of the road with a baseball bat."

"Ass," I grunt with a shadow of a smile.

"Hey, if you're gonna keep showing me up like this, I gotta get my shots in somewhere," he says as he cracks his knuckles when he can tell the scout is looking at us. "What are we gonna do with these two?"

"Leave 'em," I grunt. "Won't be nightfall before a trucker drives by and either helps 'em out or reports it. They won't be able to show their faces back with the Buzzsaws, though. Not after a humiliating ass-kicking like that. They're only prospects, they're probably looking to weed out fuckers like them."

"You're right on that," Tank says grimly, crossing his arms. "Diesel'd probably just as soon shoot 'em on suspicion that they talked." He turned to me again with a brighter smile. "Get anything juicy from 'em?"

"It's going to be an ugly war," I say bluntly. "Got 'em to admit the Buzzsaws don't seem to mind civilian casualties. They were behind Greg's brother getting hit."

"Son of a bitch," Tank grumbles, pulling his bandana off his head and running his hand through his hair. "Sure we don't want to drag 'em further off the road and let the coyotes get to them?"

"Tempting," I grunt. "We can tell Breaker we can't ignore the mayor anymore, either. If there's going to be a war, we can't have the town turned against us. The supply line is everything in a war, and if our own people don't support us, it's already over."

"Then we need them out of our hair," Tank agrees.

"And we need to smooth things over somehow," I add, frowning. "The shit with that senator's brat Brandon keeps hanging over us. Asshole is still in town. It's making us look bad."

"Maybe we should up our dress code, start riding in tuxes," Tank says with a wink, and I chuckle. "Anyway, I got news for you, too."

"Huh?" I grunt as we make our way toward the bikes slowly, not listening to the increasingly nervous scout shouting at us from the tree as he realizes we're leaving him.

"Before you told me you were running off to

chase down an unfair fight," Tank says, putting his hands on his belt, "I got a message to give you from someone who'd say you know what it means. Your ears only."

I stop dead in my tracks. There could be only one thing he meant, hedging around something so carefully like that. I turn to him slowly and hear him say the last words I'd ever want to hear, right now of all times, on the brink of a bloody war.

"Juliette is coming home."

J tilt my head back as my hands slide down my pelvis, curving over my hips and inward before dancing away. My eyes flutter open slowly, lashes trembling. I draw a deep breath, my eyes locked on the ceiling tiles fitted so precisely in ivory squares. This house has that going for it, at least. Symmetry. Normalcy. Consistency. Things never change here, never deviate from the expected. I suppose for some people that could be a nice thing. There were certainly times in my life when a little stability would've been helpful. But nowadays, it just feels like boredom to me. Which is why I have to find little moments like this, to sneak away and inject some much-needed excitement into the day. This time, I'm using the ruse of a bath for sore muscles. I grabbed a bag of Epsom salt from my mother's medicine cabinet and limped off down the hallway to the guest bathroom (in this case, I am the guest), telling my mom I must have pulled a muscle while scrubbing the dishes this morning. But the moment I slid down under the steaming, floral-scented bathwater, I felt a different part of my body was crying out for attention. And I deserve a little escape, don't I?

My hands smooth along the insides of my thighs under the surface of the pink-tinged water. I bite my lip, holding back a moan as my fingers circle inward. I let myself get so tantalizingly close and then back away again. I like to test myself, see where my limits lie. I've always been a little competitive, even if sometimes it's me I'm competing with. But right now, the last thing I should be doing is withholding from myself. I have spent enough time on other people for the time being. This alone time is sacred and elusive and I should treat it that way.

I sink lower into the bath with a deep sigh. Goosebumps prickle up on my skin. The contrast between the hot water on my abdomen and the cool air stiffening my nipples into sensitive peaks makes me feel deliciously stimulated. The worries slip away out of my mind, trickling through my memory like water through a thin sieve. The tension in my muscles starts to loosen out and dissipate, my hard-working body soothed by the warm, healing water. I part my thighs a little farther and let my fingers trail down to center on my clit. With almost agonizing slowness, I circle and back away, circle and back away. It's like dancing to the edge of a cliff only to prance back to safety. Only, I want to reach the edge. I want to topple over and free fall through the ecstatic pleasure of letting my desire take control. Maybe that's why they call it the little death. Either way, I want it. I need it. And this time, I'm going to let myself have it.

I let my mind wander as I softly caress and massage my sensitive flower, my petals blooming and tingling with every gentle touch. Wild images begin to flicker onto the projection screen of my mind. Bright flashes of vivid color and movement. Large hands roving down my body, groping my breasts and rolling my taut nipples between his fingers. The smell of smoky, well-worn black leather. The acrid burn of gasoline in my nose. The rumble of an engine shaking the earth under my feet as I watch him, the shapeshifting man of my fantasies, mounting his black motorcycle.

My eyes open and I stare up at the ceiling tiles for a moment, annoyed at myself. Why does my dream guy have to morph into a motorcycle guy? It seems to happen every single time these days, and I can't explain why. In fact, I have lots of reasons to not fantasize about that kind of man. I've had more than my fair share of trouble thanks to bikers in my life, in general. But at the same time, I can't deny how much the aesthetic appeals to me. The shiny metal, the soft leather, the musky scent, the feeling of wind whipping through my hair... I can imagine it all so colorfully. I can almost hear the tires scratching across the pavement. My eyelids shut again as I give in to the fantasy. I might as well. I'm tired of holding back-- I need this release more than anything. One of my hands trails up to caress my breasts, and I imagine what it would feel like if it were a big, manly, calloused hand instead of my soft dainty one. My other hand busies itself between my thighs, rubbing and circling as my hips rock and sway in the rhythm. It feels so damn good, every muscle in my body releasing tension as I moan and whimper in the bath.

In my mind, I'm transported far away, drifting on the winds of fantasy. Gloved hands grabbing me around the waist. Prickly jawline brushing against my ticklish neck. A harsh growl at my ear and a hard cock pressing against my side. I touch myself faster, quickening the tight circles around my clit until I'm almost gasping for air. My heart pounds faster and harder. That tautly-bound coil deep inside of me seems to burst free of its shape all at once, like a rubber band being flung across a wide chasm. My tension breaks and a climax shudders through my trembling body, making the water shake and splash with each involuntary spasm. I picture my mystery guy scooping me up and carrying me off, still twitching with release, to some highway clubhouse for a second round. Oh, what a delicious idea.

I'm still coming down from the head-spinning high of orgasm when I'm rudely interrupted by a loud buzzing sound. I sit up quickly, startled, only to realize it's just my phone vibrating on the bathroom counter. Of course. So much for a moment of peace and alone time. For a few seconds I just stare at the phone without moving. Maybe it's just a fluke. A random message. Nothing urgent that needs my immediate attention and response.

But then it vibrates again and I have to face the reality that my lovely little bath session has come to an end. I pull the bathtub plug and stand up. Goosebumps instantly poke up on my body as I grab a towel and start drying off. I pick up my phone and, sure enough, it's a couple text messages from my mother just down the hallway, requesting my assistance. Duty calls.

So I hastily towel my long black hair until it's mostly dry and fluffy, then retreat quickly to my bedroom to get dressed. I pull on a pair of tight black jeans that hug my rounded hips and taut ass, then throw on a lacy black crop top with a slightly oversized black-and-green plaid flannel shirt over it. I slip on a pair of thick black socks to combat the October cold snap raging outside the walls of our house in Laramie, Wyoming. Well, I say 'our house' but it doesn't feel much like home for me. Not for a long time. But I guess I'll just have to adjust, because Mom needs me, and I'm not going anywhere anytime soon. I stop and glance at myself in the full-length mirror hanging on the wall in my bedroom and can't help but grimace. Somehow, despite the fact that I'm twenty-five, I feel like I'm looking at the teenage version of myself. Maybe it's the context, the fact that I'm standing in my childhood bedroom. It's the second week I've been here attending to my mom's medical needs, and while it feels slightly less foreign now, it still isn't comfortable. Like wearing a shirt that technically fits, but doesn't feel right. Like there's an itchy tag or an asymmetrical hem stitch. Too tight in the chest, too boxy in the waist.

The truth is, I moved out when I was eighteen and I never really looked back. I still maintained loose contact with my mom, making sure to call her on major holidays, but that was pretty much the extent of our relationship once I left home. As soon as I could burst free of this tight little bubble of a community in nowheresville, I headed straight for Denver. It was hard work. Expensive. Stressful. Sometimes even overwhelming. But I found work as an at-home carer, utilizing my complete lack of squeamishness and my ability to chat with just about anyone from any walk of life to my advantage. My patients looked forward to my visits, even if I was only there for an hour to cook some soup and do some light physical therapy. I worked a lot of hours, and it showed. But I was willing and happy to do whatever it took to support myself and make it work out there in Denver. I craved the anonymity and endless possibilities of a big, shiny metropolis. I wanted to walk down unfamiliar streets, see unfamiliar faces. I wanted to escape the little box I grew up in. I guess it runs in my blood. We're a family of birds who do not like to be caged, we just find different ways of spreading our wings. Our own little brand of personal freedom. Mine was Denver.

But now? I don't really know. I'm still trying to get my bearings. Seven years I have been away. And yet, it feels like nothing has really changed here at all. I'm different, or at least I think I am, but it's so easy to fall back into old patterns. I walk through a room and relive every memory embedded in the floorboards and the walls and the same old furniture. I'm pushed back in time, back into the body of a seven-year-old Juliette or, even worse, sixteen-year-old Juliette. I see my mom as she once was-- seemingly healthy and on her feet, darting around the house cleaning and cooking like a domestic goddess. I don't know how she ever had the time or energy for all that. Sometimes I even wonder if all those years of hustling have caught up to her. She definitely needs a lot more help these days. Her illness isn't life-threatening, but it is chronic. It saps all her energy and makes her dizzy. The power-mom of my childhood has been slowed down to half speed. But she's my mother, and despite the distance (and the literal distance) between us for seven years, I love her with my whole heart. I wouldn't want anyone else taking care of her. Besides, I've got all the training and know-how. Might as well be me.

That's what a good daughter would do, right? I'm always trying to do the right thing. Usually, it's pretty obvious what the right thing is, at least from my experience. I trust my gut. And my gut is telling me that my mom needs me now more than ever, and I owe it to her. I just wish I had kept up closer contact with her when I moved out at eighteen. Sometimes it does get a little awkward in the house. After all, we have had seven years in the void between us. Seven years to grow out and apart. I have changed a lot. But apart from her physical illness, Mom is pretty much the same. And now that I'm back, I feel those old habits creeping up again. That diplomatic urge to fix things, to be the mediator, to put a bandage on every problem. I learned how to do that at a young age, and being back in this house reminds me of every lesson. It's wild to me how it can feel the same, and yet the soft, warm vibe I felt here as a small child is... different now. Like something has been disturbed in the air. Altered irrevocably.

The texts from my mom are strange enough-- that she's reminding me to start the preparations for dinner instead of whipping up a hearty meal in the kitchen herself. I know it must be at least as annoying for her as it is for me. After all, I know exactly from whom I inherited my need for control. I come by it honestly. But *her* overly-detailed instructions and insistence on a rigid schedule for everything does prick at my nerves just a little bit. Oh, and then there's the fact that the only thing that seems to both entertain and soothe her enough to chill out and get the bedrest her doctor insists on is a steady stream of *Jeopardy!* reruns. I've had the theme music stuck in my head since day one of my arrival here. I don't know how she stands it, but she's the one in pain, not me. If she wants to veg out with Alex Trebek, that's her prerogative. Maybe the monotony of it comforts her in some way. Who knows? As long as she's happy, I'm happy to deal with it. Besides, her game show-watching does come with a hilarious side effect: I get to hear my mom shout out her answers to the questions posed on the show. And even though my mother is a perfectly reasonable and intelligent woman, she is miraculously bad at trivia. Like, astonishingly bad. She's the opposite of a good guesser, which makes for a good bit of enter-tainment on my part.

"You going downstairs to start on dinner yet?" she calls out down the hallway as she hears the tell-tale creak of my bedroom door. Ears like a bat, that woman.

"Yes, Mom. I'm going now," I assure her, trying not to sound irritated.

I know she doesn't mean to pick and prod, but she can't help it. There's a lot to juggle around here. Between cooking, cleaning, making sure all the bills are paid on time, maintaining the small but precarious garden out back, and caring for my mom, it's a full-time job. And it's not just my mom's trivia guesses that break the quiet. For some reason beyond my understanding, my mom recently decided it would be a great idea to adopt a dog. She selected a very cute, very tiny, and very particular terrier. His name is Guacamole, and he constantly barks at me. Only at me. I don't know what it is.

Whatever the reason, Guacamole's barking is just one little facet of the stressful environment I find myself in here. Of course, it doesn't help that I'm staying in my childhood bedroom. It's hard to feel like an accomplished, capable adult when you're lying awake in the same bed you used to not-sleep in as a kid. Back then, my insomnia was probably just a symptom of my energetic personality. Not exactly what one might call bubbly, but certainly socially active. Nowadays I think it's more worry than excitement that keeps me up at night. But perhaps that's just part of growing up. We're all just doing our best-- including my mom. She really has tried to make my return home less fraught. I do wish she had taken the time to pull down all my old band posters, though. That's a little embarrassing to look at.

I hurry down to the kitchen and start taking out items on my mom's (very thorough) recipe she sent me over email. Yeah, email. I know. I listen to music and sing along under my breath, dancing around a little while I cook dinner. I do enjoy cooking-- it's a great opportunity to keep my hands busy while my mind wanders. I wash and slice up a bunch of veggies, making sure all my ingredients are prepped as I start the cooking process. I let myself get lost in the music and the rhythmic movements until something prickles at my periphery. Something worrisome. I freeze up and listen hard, tuning out the music to hear the singular but distinct click of a door opening.

For half a second, I assume it's my mom. But she's upstairs.

And that click? That's the sound the front door makes.

My heart starts to pound like crazy as I reach for a cutting knife from the block. Adrenaline starts to flood my system, and I hold my breath without meaning to. I stand perfectly still, watching the entrance to the kitchen, which is just down a short hallway from the front door of the house. I can hear my blood rushing in my ears as a long, tall shadow stretches down the wall, framed in the doorway. The breath catches in my throat and my eyes widen. I clench the handle of the knife more tightly. I'm poised to defend myself if need be.

But no sooner has that thought crossed my mind than the figure stepped through the door of the kitchen. I let out a little gasp of fear and fall back against the counter, only to immediately roll my eyes when I see who the mysterious intruder is.

"Clint! You asshole. You scared the hell out of me," I groan.

"Not my fault you're jumpy," he replies with a smirk. He sniffs the air conspicuously. "What are you making in here? Smells like roadkill."

"It's called a vegetable. I know you've never seen one of those before, but I promise it won't bite," I toss back.

"Yeah and neither will I," he murmurs.

"Don't worry. There's pasta, too," I assure him. I don't know why I feel the need to try with him, but I do. Guess that's the mediator in me.

"Good. Go light on the veggies for me, eh?" Clint says with a nudge to my shoulder.

"Who said I'm making enough for three?" I reply.

"I do. Besides, you eat too much anyway. You can spare a little for me," he jokes.

I roll my eyes. I know that's not true. He's been cracking those lines for years.

"You're tracking dirt through my clean house," I point out.

"Well, then I guess it's not a clean house anymore.

Looks like you'll be cleaning again before bed tonight," he teases.

"Great. Looking forward to it," I grumble as I turn back to tend the stove.

"Me too," he retorts. "Not that anyone even told me you were back in town, much less inviting me to dinner. You know that just breaks my heart."

I snort. "Yeah, right. Like you even have a heart to break."

He pulls a sarcastic frowny face and places a hand over his heart. "Ouch," he pouts.

"My bad," I quip.

"Yeah. Your bad," he agrees.

Half an hour later, dinner is ready and I help my mom down the stairs so we can all sit in the living room to eat. My mom is perched in a comfy, supportive armchair with a food tray and her feet propped up per the doctor's orders. That leaves Clint and me on the couch, sitting as far apart as humanly possible as we pick at dinner. It's awkward as hell, but Mom tries her best to make it nice, as usual. I see where I get it from.

"Oh, it's so lovely to have everyone back together in the same room once in a while," she remarks sweetly, looking back and forth between us with genuine affection.

"Yeah, well, we'd do it more often if Juliette hadn't skipped town on us, huh?" Clint snaps back, casting a cruel glance my way. I glare right back at him.

"I've been back for over a week. You could've come by earlier," I remind him.

He flicks his gaze back to Mom. "And you know, I've been real busy with the club."

Mom brightens up, trying to warm to his topic. "Oh, that's nice. How is the, uh, motorcycle thing going?" she asks.

I have to resist the urge to laugh. Clint looks prickly at her reductive phrasing for a moment, but he shakes it off.

"Long rides and lots of dinners on the road," he replies coolly. "You know, this meal actually reminds me of some of the skeeziest diners I've stopped at."

"Gee, thanks," I groan, rolling my eyes. "It's still free food, you know."

"Well, yeah. You certainly couldn't charge a dime for this mess," he teases.

It doesn't bother me. Truthfully, Clint's comments slide off like water off a duck's backside. I have enough self-confidence to not let his barbed criticisms cut deep. But it's still grating on my nerves, and as usual, Mom doesn't say or do a thing to stop him. She never does. I know he's the favorite, after all. He continues to be an ass throughout dinner, but the conversation remains mostly civil. At the end, I help Mom get back upstairs and she reminds me to lock up after Clint leaves. Just like always, he gets to be irresponsible and I have to make it right. Some things never change.

I hurry back downstairs just as Clint is pulling on his leather jacket to leave. Now that we're out of earshot of Mom, it's my turn to throw daggers. I quirk an eyebrow and cross my arms over my chest, watching him shrug into his sleeves.

"Nice jacket. You still going to put that ridiculous bull-ring back in before you get back to your man-club, Clint?" I jab. "Or wait-- is it still Diesel now or have you been downgraded to Premium Unleaded?"

"Hilarious," he quips, throwing me a middle finger as he walks out the door. He glances back at me and adds, "You're lucky you're my little sister."

I give him the bird right back. "Luck has nothing to do with it," I reply.

It's been a week since she's been back home, give or take, and this town is small enough that when an out-of-state license plate like hers sticks around, it stands out. A warm breeze ruffles the tattered kutte hanging on my shoulders as my bike idles under me. I watch her sleek car fly past the highway below the hill I'm keeping watch from, off a dirt road from which I can see those tags clearly in the late morning light. I don't even need to check them. A glance in the window is all I need.

It's her, alright. I'd never forget that face.

The last time I'd seen her, we'd just been kids, but I'd still had a heart back then like I have a heart now. I just put on a little more muscle to house it, but it never forgot Diesel's little sister Juliette. I never told anyone about the day we crossed paths, but it had stuck with me. We barely even talked to each other. I doubt she'd remember me out of the sea of bikers, but that's fine by me.

She doesn't need to know I'm watching for me to keep her safe.

Once she's far enough ahead of me on the road, I slowly roll down the dirt path to the highway and get back on asphalt. I start tailing her from a distance, and I can keep a hell of a distance, thanks to how much her car stands out on the open roads and plains. Besides, I've tailed people before, even out here where you have to hide in plain sight. She won't see me unless I want to be seen.

I've been keeping tabs on her indirectly over the years, but now that she's back in Wyoming, I want to see what she's up to. Once she gets into town, I see her park at a bank and head inside. When she gets out, even from a distance, I'm struck by the sight of her.

Changed isn't the right word for her. More like blossomed. She's even more beautiful than I remember her, and considering the way she appears in my sweetest memories, shining and full of light despite her dark aesthetic, that's saying something. We may have been kids back then, but the woman in a warm cardigan, jeans, and comfortable boots all in the same shade of inky black as her hair looks more like herself than even my memories tell me.

It takes everything in me not to rocket over to that parking lot, cut her off halfway to the doors, and tell her to saddle up, because I'm taking her home. For a worrying second, it actually doesn't sound like the worst idea, considering the storm brewing for the MC.

But I keep my distance several blocks down, and when she keeps going, I follow.

The route takes her to a grocery store, a pharmacy, and a few other odds and ends that add up to a whole hell of a lot of errands. She looks more stressed out with each place she goes to. She spent more time in the pharmacy than anywhere else, and through the window, I could see an exasperated silhouette at the counter and a large number of pill bottles getting shuffled around between her and the pharmacist.

I don't know her life *that* closely, but I'm fairly sure I'd have known by now if she were the kind of person who needed that many medications, and it seemed like there was a lot of explaining going on in there. To me, all that pointed to was that she was running someone *else's* errands.

Family must be involved here. And that's bad, because family means Diesel, and Diesel means death.

I can't see it any other way. She's got to get out of here, no matter what she's here for.

A little after lunch time, just long enough that my own stomach is starting to growl and get me restless, she pulls into a gas station on the outskirts of town across the street from a burger joint whose freshly grilling meat makes my gut roar. I slow down as I approach, meaning to pull over behind the restaurant parking lot, but something else at the gas station gets my attention.

Juliette has the gas nozzle in her car, but there's a huge truck with four back tires and a set of truck nuts swinging under the hitch at the one opposite her. Standing around it are four local guys, probably none of them older than twenty, all in thick blue jeans and boots and camo long sleeve shirts. A couple of them are even wearing caps with a hunting logo on them.

I don't have to be close to know they're checking her out, and I know the looks on their faces. I see one of them calling to her, and as I near the turn to pull into the gas station, I see Juliette noticeably tense up and avoid eye contact as they start to try to get her attention.

"Hey there pretty little thing, you look friendly!"

"Ain't seen you before, new around here?"

"Gonna get hot in all that black, sweetie!"

Revving my bike as I coast into the lot while they call at her, I slowly rolled up between the two gas pumps, giving the local boys a stony glare as I came to a full stop. As my boot hits the ground, all of them have their eyes on me, and they can see my kutte just fine where they are. One by one, their faces pale at the sight of me, and after a few quick looks to each other, most of them pile back into the truck. The driver averts his eyes but gives a curt nod in my direction as he gets into his seat, and their eyesore of a ride roars off.

I watch them go before the feeling of being watched makes me turn around.

The gaze that met me hits harder than any of those local boys put together could have.

She has warm brown eyes that are so dark they might be black, like everything else she's got on her--just like everything I've got on me, for that matter. The slight curls that spiral at the ends of the hair that hangs well past her shoulders make me want to run my thick fingers through them and ask her whether she remembers the coal-black eyes looking back at her.

I know she does. It's written all over her face, in the surprised silence that hangs between us. That gaze flits all over my body, and the surprise on it isn't the same kind of surprise as when you see a stranger. She wasn't expecting to see me, all right, but I wonder if the memory of *me* has aged as well as mine of her.

But the second she realizes she's staring, a faint blush crosses her cheeks, and her full lips turn down in a frown as she furrows her brow.

"You a friend of my brother's? He didn't send you to follow me, did he? I noticed you after the grocery store, tell *Diesel* he can fuck off."

"Friend of Diesel's?" I ask, chuckling darkly. "Not for a long, long time."

The hostility in her eyes seems to fade, but she still looks suspicious. I can't blame her. I'm not the most trusting guy myself, either.

"So what, you know him but you're not close?" she asks, arching an eyebrow. After a tense pause, she cracks a shadow of a smile. "Well in that case, you sound alright. Thanks."

I couldn't help but snort a laugh at that, and my heart races, but she's not so quick to warm up.

"But then why were you following me?" she asks. "...and why do you look so familiar?"

"So you *do* recognize me," I say, and when she answers only with that steady, suspicious gaze, I nod across the street to the restaurant. "Yeah, I know Diesel. And we need to talk. Let me buy you lunch. For your trouble," I add, nodding to where the truck nuts crew had been.

Her gaze is hard to read for a few moments, but finally, she gives a soft nod. "Alright. Half an hour, no more. I've got to get back home."

"This place is fast," I assure her.

A few minutes later, she's staring at me with a raised eyebrow across the booth at the burger joint after putting in a couple of easy orders. "*Big Daddy?*"

"Didn't choose it," I grunt. "Long story. Besides, I'm here to talk about Diesel, not me."

She seems to have relaxed a little the more clear it becomes that I've actually got something to tell her, and that I didn't just swoop in to snatch her up for a cheap date. That just happened to be a perk on the side.

"Oh my god, I was joking earlier," she says, grinning. "Does he seriously still have everyone call him that?"

It's hard not to laugh, despite the fact that this is a damn serious matter. Even though I've always known Juliette as Diesel's sister, it never really struck me that she must know a side of him I've never seen or even thought possible. The Diesel I know is singlehandedly responsible for the spike in sex trafficking and murders across the Great Plains that we've been fighting back for months.

The Diesel she knows might well be the boy she grew up with.

"Yeah," I say simply. "We use our riding names for club business."

"And you'd say you know my brother in a business way?" she asks, folding her arms in front of her and tilting her head to the side.

She seems at least interested in her brother, and if that's keeping her attention, all the better. I wonder how much they've kept up over the years.

"You could say that," I say, resting my fist in my hand as I lean on the table. "The last time you saw us together--the last night we met--was one of the last times we were in the same room together. You remember that night?"

"Hard to forget my own eighteenth birthday," she says smoothly with a joyless, sarcastic smile that tells me it was anything but a happy one. "My mom had guilted me into visiting him out in Table Rock on *my* birthday because *he* wouldn't come up again that year. Yeah, I know, TMI, I'm not bitter," she added.

"Damn, I remember it was your birthday, but I didn't know that," I said with raised eyebrows.

She seems to notice the first part of that sentence, and I could have sworn her eyes soften just a hint at it. I didn't even think about it when I let it slip, but how could I have forgotten?

"Yeah, my brother had...promised me a drink or two under the table," she said, averting her eyes for a moment but hiding any more embarrassment. "Said it was practically his place, he could do whatever he wanted there."

"I bet he did say that," I grunt.

"Without mentioning making me pay for them," she added with a tight smile that soon softened. "You were-" she stopped herself and started again. "You getting the tab was honestly the nicest surprise of the day, sad as that sounds, so thanks for that."

She said it almost sardonically, but she averted her eyes as she spoke and ran a hand through a lock of hair as she looked up to the two massive burgers getting carried over to us and set down in front of us, making both our eyes widen.

I nod to the waiter, but my eyes are still on Juliette, and my heart is racing. This is almost too good to believe, but Juliette seems to remember me a lot more than I expected her to. I didn't even know she knew I'd covered her drinks for her that night. Diesel had just been an enforcer back then, and I'd thought of him as a scummy dick for the way he treated the knockout who had walked through the doors to see him.

Hiding how much the memory had stuck with me all these years almost made me forget the way she held my attention whenever her eyes were on me. I could have picked her up effortlessly, and I had half a mind to do so, but I felt like I was spellbound.

"Well, happy birthday," I say with a shadow of a gruff smile.

A hint of color crosses her cheeks before we start eating. Despite the joking, the way she looks at me is as suspicious as I'd expect anyone to be after getting pulled into a diner with a biker my size. I can barely leave the clubhouse without the dense tattoos covering my sleeves from shoulder to wrist drawing looks.

"But that was a long time ago, Juliette," I said after we'd scarfed down enough to shut our stomachs up and slow down. "A *long* time. Me and my friends, we split from the Buzzsaws."

"And that's...Diesel's gang?" she asks between bites, narrowing her eyes.

"You two don't keep up much, do you?" I ask, and she shakes her head. "Yeah, sort of. That was the old Buzzsaws, but the new ones are worse, and they're the ones your brother is tied to."

The last two words of that are a lie of omission, I'll admit.

How could I tell Juliette her brother is the leader of a sex-trafficking biker gang? Would I believe that about my own brother if a stranger told me? I have to measure every word carefully here. I can tell she's not the type that scares easily.

As a guy people call scary, I can appreciate that trait in a woman.

"I'm not going to bullshit you, Juliette," I say, lowering my voice in the din of the bustling diner's lunch rush so that only the two of us can hear us talking. "The Buzzsaws are bad people. Real fucking bad. And they're not friends with me and my people."

Her eyes slowly widen, and I notice her almost easy posture start to grow tense as she watches me suspiciously before swallowing a bite. "So...you're from a rival biker gang?"

"Easy, it isn't what you're thinking," I say, holding up a large open hand. "If I had a problem with you, you'd know--I don't. We're having this conversation because *you* are in danger."

"Me?" is the vague sound she makes through a closed mouthful of food, looking surprised, then swallowing. "Why me? I-I'm not a biker, I don't even know anything about this stuff. I live in Denver, I'm just visiting here to take care of my mom. She's...not doing great," she says, trying to sound mild, but I can sense the thick layers of stress and worry in her tone.

They're so strong she can barely hide them. So, she's here to take care of family after all. That makes sense. From what I've kept up about her, I last heard she was working as some kind of caretaker herself. She'd be the perfect person for a sick parent to want nearby. And that explains the errands...as well as the stress that I can sense crackling around her like tight static electricity. She must be under an enormous amount of pressure.

I can't say I know what it's like to have a parent to care for, but it clearly means a lot to her. That can't change things, though. She needs to get out of here.

"Because people who are close to the Buzzsaws get hurt, Juliette," I say bluntly. "And you're Diesel's sister. That means something, more than you want to know."

Those last words were probably a mistake, but maybe I just have a hard time keeping the girl I've been waiting to talk to for seven long years in the dark.

"Is this some kind of threat?" she asks, lowering her burger.

"It's a warning," I say firmly, leaning forward. "I'm giving it to you straight because we're both adults now, Juliette--the Buzzsaws are doing bad shit, and my people are trying to stop them. It's going to turn hot, and we're not the ones making the first move. They are. Including your brother," I say slowly, so she doesn't misunderstand a word of what I'm saying.

Unfortunately, she doesn't, but neither does she seem to like what I'm saying.

"So yeah, a threat," she says, furrowing her brow.

"I'm trying to look out for you, Juliette," I say, lowering my voice but putting more force behind it.

"I don't need anyone to look out for me," she snaps, jabbing a thumb at herself. "*I'm* the one looking out for *my* family. It always has been, and it always will be. And look, I know you've got your gang rivalry or whatever, but my brother isn't *that* stupid!"

"No, he's not," I say, trying not to sound impatient, but the tension between us has shifted, and it's impossible to ignore. "That's my point, Juliette. Your brother knows exactly what he's doing, and it's going to get you hurt. You need to go back to Denver."

"You don't know what I need to do," she says matter of factly. "I don't even know how you found me, but what I need to do is look out for my people. Thanks for the help with the assholes, but despite your name, *you're not my daddy*, so don't act like it," she finishes pointedly.

You want to change that, little girl?

The silence that hangs between us for a moment seems to have something similar on her mind too, because I see the goosebumps on her arm even though her brow is set.

"You think your brother is your people, Juliette," I say slowly in a low, gravelly voice. "He's not. And you need to stay away from him."

"I can handle myself, thanks," she says, getting up from her seat after wiping her hands off on a napkin and picking her purse up, glaring at me, cheeks burning. "And I can do that without some biker's thoughts on my family."

She storms out of the diner, leaving me calmly watching her leave. She throws the door open and marches down to her car while I casually wipe my own hands off, toss the napkin down, and laid a $50 on the table, giving a nod to the server nearby.

I seem to have struck a raw nerve, to put it lightly. Since Diesel was part of that nerve, that makes this a little more complicated. I don't want to have to take more extreme measures than this. I hoped she'd see reason--one conversation with her is all I need to know she's smart as hell, just like I remember. I'm used to women looking up at me all doe-eyed. Juliette has fire in her, and she's not afraid to use it.

In all the time I'd had to stew on that memory of her, I'd never been more into her than now.

As her car roars off, I watch her go until she's out of sight, then take my phone out of my pocket and give Tank a call.

"Hey," I grunt. "Listen, I need to call in that favor we talked about. This one stays between us. And you're going to get the hard part, so take notes."

I feel like there might as well be steam coming out of my ears, I am so angry. I fume as I walk briskly out of the diner and get in my car. I jam the key in the ignition and fire up the engine, all but peeling out in my haste to put distance between myself and that jerk. I can't believe the nerve of him, accusing my brother of being some heartless villain. Who the hell does he think he is? I have no reason to believe anything he says. He doesn't know jack shit about my family. I almost wish I had stayed a little longer at lunch, though. Just long enough to tell him off. Instead, I just mumble angrily to myself as I make the drive home.

"What does he know?" I grumble, shaking my head. My knuckles are white curled over the steering wheel. I force myself to take a deep breath.

I know the truth. Right? My brother may not be

the nicest guy you could ever meet. I mean, he's been a biker for god knows how long. For all I know, that clubhouse he hangs around could be filled with rough characters who are most definitely a bad influence on him. I'm not totally naive. I'm well aware that some bikers do get into serious stuff. But not Clint. Not my brother. I can't even entertain the idea. The cheeky bastard who rolled up to our childhood home to startle me and criticize my cooking while tracking mud through the clean house is no more than that: a cheeky bastard. He's just another fabric in the unchanged tapestry of this town and the memories I built here. Just like the house creaks and settles the same way I remember it growing up, my brother is the same. A little rougher around the edges, worn away by years of gritting his teeth on the highway, no doubt tons of sleepless nights and hard rides.

But I still remember the lanky beanpole he was as a teenager. The goofy, rebellious, sarcastic big brother who used to blow through the house like a tornado, leaving a trail of chaos in his wake. The loud music he used to blast from his bedroom, which shook and trembled the floors and kept me awake at night. I remember the nights when he would sneak out the window, drop down to the front yard, and run off into the dark with some of those unruly friends of his.

So, sure. He's no angel. But that doesn't mean

that guy in the restaurant has any idea what he's talking about. He seemed awfully confident about his assumptions regarding my family, which naturally pissed me off. I've always been the kind of girl who likes to form my own opinion. I don't rely on what random guys tell me I should believe, even if they are ruggedly handsome, undeniably charming, and impressively muscled. Even if I can still give myself the shivers just thinking about the heat rolling off his powerful body, the faint masculine scent of him, the way his intense gaze penetrated straight through to my very soul.

Okay, admittedly my little lunchtime chat with Big Daddy might have done more than just incense my self-righteous rage. Sitting so close to him reminded me just exactly why my fantasies tend to be studded with these big, burly biker guys. There's just something about them that draws me in. Despite Clint's involvement in the scene. Or maybe because of it?

"Oof," I murmur to myself.

I decide not to go there. Not right now. I have other things to do. I have a relative at home who needs my help, so maybe this isn't the best time to psychoanalyze my sexual fantasies and try to pinpoint their origins in adolescence. That's a path to wander down some day in the eventual future when I'm *not* sleeping in my childhood home, in my childhood bed. Besides, it's not like I have time to entertain a suitor or whatever. I haven't had time for anything like love for a while now. I keep myself busy, I guess. It's just easier that way. I've been let down and disappointed by too many men in my twenty-five years to give them any more opportunities.

So I won't let myself dwell on how badly my body aches to be closer to Big Daddy. Isn't that basically like dating my brother anyway? I mean, he used to run with a similar crowd. I have a clear memory of him on a specific and fateful night when I was seventeen years old. Back then, I was just on the cusp of spreading my wings and taking to the sky. I was still a bird in her cage, wings kept neatly tucked down at her sides. I was trying to be a dutiful daughter, but I was fed up. I was tired of seeing the same old places, same old faces. I wanted more than my little hometown could offer, and that restlessness I probably inherited from my father pulsed hotly in my veins. I was seventeen, but teetering on the brink of eighteen.

In fact, that very night my dear brother and wonderful influence Clint managed to sneak me into one of the bars he and his friends frequented here in town, it was my birthday. I felt dizzy. I felt antsy. Like the balls of my feet were itching to hit the pavement and flat-out run away from everything I knew and thought I understood. I was usually so well-behaved, but on that night I let myself go a little bit. I loosened the chains, just for a little while. My brother had even charitably offered to secure me a drink under the table despite my still being under-age. And he did-- he got me a drink. But the asshole left me to pay for it, which was a problem considering I was just a kid at the time and didn't have a penny to my name. That night, I had been assured that Clint would take care of everything. Not very convincingly assured, but still. I expected he would buy me a soda or lemonade and let me hang around the pool tables while he and his friends played solids and stripes. My goal was just to get through a night without drama or trouble. I wanted a smooth, normal eighteenth birthday… with maybe a little dash of measured excitement if possible. What I did not expect was to be stuck with a cocktail bill, standing dumbly at the bar clutching the tab with wide eyes and shaking hands.

As I'm remembering this embarrassing moment in my teendom, it hits me that someone did step up to save me. And it wasn't nobody, either. It was Big Daddy. Through the cloud of time and bashfulness I had all but forgotten about his princely act of paying my tab. He didn't make a big deal out of it. He just snaked the bill from my hand and slid it across the bar counter with a wad of cash that far exceeded the price and tip. And then he disappeared again into the crowd, just as seamlessly as he had appeared. I remember feeling both confused and relieved, but not just that-- I was disappointed. I wanted to at least tell him thank you. But I could tell he didn't want my praise. He did it because it was a good thing to do. A helpful thing. And now, as I drive home from our heated lunch discussion, I can't help but wonder how long he's been looking out for me that way.

I can't believe I let it slip my mind. Such a simple gesture, but it saved my night. Obviously, I'm not about to declare Big Daddy a saint just based on that one act. I'm not innocent enough to believe he makes a habit of rescuing damsels from unpaid bar tabs. It was probably a fluke. He's not my guardian angel. He's not my actual daddy. He's just an exceedingly hot guy who just so happened to do me a favor years ago... and is also probably the reason I imprinted on and grew attached to the fantasy of loving a biker guy. I remember the way he exuded a cool confidence even back then. Those muscles and that assertive, no-nonsense way of making things right; I can't pretend like I'm not totally drawn to that package.

But no. I remind myself that I don't need someone to take care of me. I am not a helpless damsel. I'm an independent young woman who can handle my own messes. It's totally presumptuous and unfair of him to think otherwise. Am I not handling my mom's medical issues with grace? Am I not running the household efficiently? I know who I am and what I'm doing. I'm good on my own. Even if the idea of being protected and rescued by a guy like Big Daddy turns me on beyond belief. I have to keep my head on straight. No distractions.

Still, though, as I drive home I can't help but wonder if maybe I do have my blinders up when it comes to my family. More specifically, my brother. After all, he's always been a charmer. Wicked but charismatic, a deadly combination. It dawns on me that he's not really much like the Clint I grew up with. It's like he's buried that version of himself deep, deep in the plains of Wyoming. Scattered his old self along the dusty highways, whittling himself down to the sharpened edge he is now. No longer just Clint… he's Diesel now. The world knows him that way. I know Clint, but I'm not so sure I know Diesel. Or that I even want to.

And I do feel a little pinch of guilt at that. He's still my brother. I should care about his whereabouts and his whatbouts. I should want to know what kind of mischief he's been getting into, at least so that I might have some small chance of righting his wrongs.

"There I go again," I sigh.

The diplomat. The fixer. The one who cleans up everyone else's messes. It's like a compulsion or something. Why can't I just let sleeping dogs lie? Besides, I don't have a stake in his world anymore. I rescinded my right to that when I disappeared seven years ago. It's sad to admit, but I kept up with Diesel even less frequently than my mom when I left. As in, not really any communication at all. That was unfair of me. But then, he didn't exactly reach out to me either. It's a two-way street, I have to remind myself for the millionth time.

And yet, I find the cogs turning in my head as I pull into the driveway at home. I recall that Diesel mentioned "checking in on some buddies at the Muffler," which I knew to be the name of a rather notorious biker bar here in town. Maybe he and his new crew of ruffians could be hanging around there. Maybe I could turn up surreptitiously and just do a little light recon. A little research, just so I'm not totally out of the loop.

I walk into the house with my mind all buzzing. I have some duties to deal with here at home, taking care of my mom and everything. But beyond that, maybe my duties lie elsewhere. What if Diesel really has fallen into trouble and he just needs a helping hand? I know I can never live with myself if I pass up the chance to save someone I used to love so much. And even if he's not in jeopardy, I might get to see my brother in his natural environment and learn a little about who he's become. I have this deep-seated sense of obligation to get to know my remaining family members, to make up for the seven lost years in between. I have a lot to answer for, and perhaps this could be the next step. I make the quiet decision to go out to the Muffler later, once things are stable at home.

I keep my plan to myself, even while my mom and I hang out downstairs and chat as I do chores. That's one I do appreciate about my mom nowadays. She trusts me to do my own thing for the most part, as long as I keep up with running the household, of course. Maybe it's a side effect of raising a kid like my brother, who was constantly pushing back and fighting for more control and freedom. He and my mom butted heads up until the point when her patience ran out and she gave up. I remember how defeated she looked after their shouting matches. She wanted so badly to understand and relate to him, but he would never let any of us in. Not really. I try my best to make up for Diesel's lack. Mom and I talk about inconsequential things. The weather. The heat. Meatloaf recipes. House repairs. It's pleasant and enjoyable enough to keep me almost distracted while I cook dinner that night, but not quite. I have been anxiously watching the seconds tick down on the clock, inching closer to the hour of my little Muffler mission. Once dinner is done, the dishes are clean, and I've eased my mom carefully up the stairs to her bedroom, I quietly pad off to my own bedroom to change out of my slouchy pajamas and into a more bar-appropriate outfit.

I'm not totally sure what the dress code is like for a biker bar these days, but I decide on a form-fitting black dress I got at a thrift store back in Denver. It has a slightly-frayed lacy trim, which I make look more intentional by adding an almost equally-frayed lacy black bralette underneath. The well-worn sides are clearly visible through the low-hanging cut of the dress. I add a pair of black tights with a considerable snag in the left thigh, a pair of dark green lace-up sneakers I've had for years, and a black duster that falls just around my ankles. I give myself a look in the mirror and wince at the mess of my hair. I tug it down from its ponytail, quickly drag a comb through it, and brush it over my shoulders, letting it fall in shiny, softened waves. I dab on some tinted lip balm and a little dash of mascara before calling it. I don't like to spend too much time in front of the mirror. I know what I look like. Any extra time I could spend doing something productive is wasted on agonizing over any imperfections I may have. I like to think I've got style, but I'm not very invested in what other people think of it.

Except for maybe Big Daddy, which is exactly what I think as I walk into the crowded, smoky lounge of the Muffler later that night. There are lots of biker guys in here. All the boots, the leather, the windswept hair, the tattoos, the pure machismo and muscle everywhere I look is enough to make any girl a little dizzy. But every time when I get a closer look, without fail, the men come up short. It's not their fault. In fact, I might usually think more highly of them. The truth is that Big Daddy reminded me what exactly it is I love about biker men. He's the prime example, and none of these guys can even come close. The bar is set too high for these chumps.

Not for lack of trying on their part, though. I can't help but notice all the turning heads as I saunter through the hazy bar to the counter. I'm confident enough to know they're all watching me. I've been getting ogled by men since long before it was appropriate for them to do so. I know what it looks like when a man's eyes light up for a pretty girl. I know how it feels to have multiple sets of eyes scrutinizing your every measurement and move. And I know the little chuckles and whispers men make when they see something they like. But I'm not here to flirt with a boy in faded jeans and scuffed-up boots. I'm on a mission. That doesn't mean I can't use their interest in me for my interest in Diesel's secret life. I sidle up to a couple of guys at the bar counter. I have to feel it out, make sure they don't know who I am. That could blow my cover. So I don't give my name. In fact, I offer as little real information as I can. It's all about bargaining. How I can get the most out of my unwitting interviewee as I can without sacrificing too much of my own. I ask seemingly innocent questions, more generally about the crowd here and who's usually around. But my biker guys give unsatisfying answers. They keep it as vague as I do, to my dismay. And once they finally realize that I'm not going to sleep with them, they sneer.

"Disrespectful, a woman asking questions like that," one of them quips.

"Excuse me?" I scoff.

"Just saying. You shouldn't be nosin' around in a mess that doesn't belong to you," says the other guy. "Don't know what you're talking about."

"Now, you want to stay and play nice, little girl?" growls the first guy.

He reaches out a grimy paw for my thigh and I slap it away. Disgusted, I stand up so quickly the bar stool topples over with a loud clatter. Everyone stops for a split second and looks over at me. Stricken with panic, the adrenaline pumps through my veins and I rush out of the bar without a glance back. Tears burn in my eyes as I dart through the small parking lot to my car. I just want to get out of here. But before I can even reach my door, I hear the heart-stopping crunch of boots hitting the gravel in heavy, rapid footsteps behind me.

Finally, I do look back. And to my horror, I see that the guy who reached for my leg is tailing me. Closely. Even worse, we appear to be alone in the parking lot. No witnesses. I gulp hard, stumbling backward. My heart is pounding. Oh, I've really screwed up this time. I try to stagger away from him but the guy lunges toward me, a cold deadness in his dark eyes. I clench my eyes shut for the tackle but a moment later I'm surprised by the softness of a hand on my arm. I open my eyes and am stunned to see Big Daddy looming beside me, almost over me. Like a protective shield against the world. Against the guy who followed me.

Big Daddy shoves something at me-- a rectangle.

"Your card," he says loudly. "You left it at the bar, tab open and everything, babe."

"Babe," I repeat in a soft voice, confused.

His eyes dart ever so briefly over at the guy who tailed me, who has shrunken back from us, obviously in light of Big Daddy showing up.

"We've got to get your memory checked out, sweetheart," he says.

I catch on. He's pretending to be my big, strong, capable boyfriend to deter my assailant.

"Oh gosh, you're so right. Thanks for checking on me, Daddy," I tell him sweetly.

I watch with relief as the drunken guy shuffles off in a huff. I look up at Big Daddy, totally unsure of whether I wanted to thank him or slap him.

"You saved me," I breathe. "But you followed me!"

He sighs. "Yes. I followed you. For your own good, clearly."

"I don't need your protection," I shoot back.

"Let's see: you immediately ran off to a biker bar all by yourself, pissed off some violent guys, made a scene, and almost fell into real trouble in the parking lot," Big Daddy lists off. "There's no way you can be here when the war gets hot."

"The war?" I murmur. "What are you even talking about?"

"It's not for you to know," he says.

Anger flashes in my chest like white-hot heat. "How the hell do you expect me to trust you?" I demand to know.

He looks at me hard for a moment, then shakes his head and reaches into his coat pocket. I flinch, expecting some kind of weapon. I see a flicker of something like pity cross his face, and then he hands me an envelope.

"What's this about?" I ask.

"First class ticket back to Denver," he replies. "Take it. Fly home."

"I am home," I insist bitterly.

"Not anymore. This isn't safe territory for you, Juliette. Believe me," he presses.

"Believe you? How? Why?" I retort.

I thrust the envelope back at him and swivel around to open my car door. To my surprise, he lets me get into my car and drive away. He watches balefully until he disappears from my rearview mirror. I drive home in a fuming rage, made even more annoyed by the way my body is reacting in contradiction with my mind. I'm pissed off. But my body? All my body wants is for me to do a U-turn and drive right back to Big Daddy.

I resist the urge. I get home and rush inside to do the remaining dishes. It's a calming activity for me, helps me clear my head. After some time, it hits me that I was in such a rush earlier I forgot to bring my purse in from the car. I dry my hands, put on my sneakers, and head back out to the car to grab it before I head upstairs for bed.

But I barely make it halfway to my car before I feel the jolt of a large hand clap over my face and a damp cloth blotting out the world into darkness.

BIG DADDY

How could I have slept last night, knowing the girl I'd stolen was just down the hall?

My bare chest has goosebumps on it in the crisp morning air as I lower my body to the floor carefully in a push-up, then repeat over and over again in my usual morning workout routine.

A little kidnapping is no excuse not to stay in shape. In fact, I think I'll need to be in the best shape I can if I want to keep a hold of Juliette.

When I grabbed her last night, it broke my heart to feel her body go tense and then limp in the arms I knew she somehow recognized, I just knew it. She didn't expect me to pull something like that, or she wouldn't have gone out last night. But I'd been tailing her all day, and the fact that she turned around and went sleuthing on her own like that tells me she's most definitely the kind of trouble I was worried about.

She's going to get herself killed, asking questions around a biker bar like that. This is for her own good. She doesn't know it yet, and she might hate me for the rest of my life for this, but if that's what it takes to keep her safe then so be it.

The Buzzsaws have taken too many lives. I don't want this one getting hurt, too. She doesn't deserve this. She deserves a happy life far, far away from all this bloodshed. I'm going to take her back to that kicking and screaming if I have to.

We're in the Black Hills just over the state line, deep in the woods where I have a safehouse lined up that only the four of us original members know about, if the other three even remember. This is hidden.

My muscles are swollen and loosened up as I rise to my feet and pull a simple black t-shirt over my torso, rolling my shoulders back as I feel the dull, warm burn of the workout in every muscle. The room that passes for a living room in this one-bedroom cabin in the middle of the woods is a surprisingly useful workout spot. I wanted to give her the bed to herself.

She might have given me no choice but to take this step, but at least I can try to make it comfortable for her.

I see the sky getting lighter outside with every

passing minute, and as the dawn passes into morning, I decide it's time to check on her. I haven't heard her stir yet, but she had a late night last night, so that's understandable.

Before I do, though, I decide a peace offering is in order. I'm not much of a cook, but the kitchenette here has a stove, and I brought supplies that includes breakfast, so as long as everything works, I can get us something going. After a few minutes cleaning off a dusty skillet and some utensils, I melt the butter, crack the eggs, feel my stomach rumble at the sizzle, and fire up a second skillet for the bacon.

It isn't elegant, but after a few minutes, I've got a whole-ass plate of protein piled high in a bowl with a garnish of thick cuts of bacon, cheese, and a side of hot sauce, just in case. I finished it off with a couple of hash browns on the side, or rather, the closest thing I'd managed to make to that with the potato and oil I was armed with.

Making sure one more time that all the doors were locked, I made my way down the short hallway past the half bathroom (the bedroom en suite is nicer, frankly) to the single bedroom, and I put my ear to it. I'm good at keeping quiet when I move, despite my size, but she could be too. After I'm fairly sure she's either still asleep or listening quietly enough that she deserves a shot at me, I unlock the door quietly and open it.

My heart nearly skips a beat at the sight of her.

She's on her back, head tilting to the side, and the warm morning sunlight coming in through the window hits her face and casts a pale glow on her hair that shows me that what I thought was black curls are actually a dark, rich brown. She seems so peaceful in the bed that I don't want to wake her. The longer she's sleeping peacefully like that, the longer it'll actually feel like I'm her protector, not the captor she's about to think I am.

No avoiding that, though.

I set the heavy bowl of breakfast on the night-stand next to her, and I carefully lean in just enough to whisper to her. "Juliette."

I see her lip twitch and curl upward, to my surprise, and she turns over in her sleep. She lets out a soft sigh, and I watch her body curl up and squirm softly under the sheets. Now I *definitely* don't want to wake her. But as she murmurs in her sleep, that groggy, cracking, soft, almost whimpering sound of her voice makes my cock pulse gently and start to swell. Fuck, even in the moments when she looks like a living work of art, she gets me going. I need to get a hold of myself.

But it's tempting to just let her go and see where this dream she seems to be having takes her. Her mouth falls open, and the way her thighs are moving...

Her eyes crack open, and I sit back slowly, furrowing my brow as she blinks a few times, then turns her tired eyes up and stares directly at me through bleary, half-closed eyelids. The gears almost visibly turn in her head for a few silent seconds before her eyes spring wide open. She bolts upright as if I'd just hit her with an adrenaline shot, and one of her arms shoots out to grab mine.

The first thing out of her mouth is not what I'm expecting.

"*Shit I over slept! My mom has to take her medication at-*" she starts to blurt, but I'm ready for this one.

"Seven thirty at the latest, half an hour ago, when she takes half of her medications, and then another round of the rest immediately after a high fiber breakfast served at eight o'clock sharp," I say smoothly, nodding.

She stares at me blankly for a few moments, more surprised by my first words as she is of mine.

"The instructions you wrote to yourself were in your car," I explain. "I've got a good friend taking care of it. Your mom is fine," I say in a low, soothing voice.

But Juliette's eyes have already started flitting around the room, and they're clearly processing what they see in the way I was worried she would. The grip on my arm suddenly tightens, and I catch her other arm's wrist just in time before she can throw a punch at me, and she starts fighting and trying to wrench away from me at the same time.

"Where the hell am I?!" she shouts. "How did you

get me here? I didn't come home with you, I remember that much!"

"You nearly got yourself in a world of hurt, little girl," I growl as I stand up and wrestle her back down to the bed, careful to keep her from hurting herself more than anything. I can take a few stray knees to my side or fists to my leg that gets away from me, I'm more likely to accidentally hurt her here. She's scared and confused, and I know I need to be patient, even though I must look like anything but the patient voice of reason in the situation.

"Yeah, from *you*, apparently!" she snaps, and I finally let go of her to let her scramble back across the bed until her back hits the wooden wall, and her chest rises and falls with quick, shallow breaths as she glares at me.

With the sheets off, she can see that she's fully clothed, and I hope that at least gives her some hope about my intentions. That doesn't change the true fact that she's not here by choice, though.

"I'm not going to hurt you," I say, slowly reaching for the bowl of breakfast. "Look, you've had a long night. You're going to want to eat something before you do anything else. Panicking takes energy."

Even I can hear her stomach growl as she sees and smells the hearty bowl of breakfast, and she definitely knows I heard. She scowls at me, then slowly extends her hands for the bowl before taking it and retreating to the wall again, glaring at me, but picking through the food with the spoon I stuck in it.

"What is this?" she asks.

"Eggs, meat, cheese," I say matter-of-factly. "I'd have a biscuit to go with, but I was short on time."

"Is my mom really okay?" she demands without missing a beat. "What did you mean, a good friend? Who's at my mom's house?"

I take out my phone and pull up the picture Tank sent me earlier this morning--a selfie of him crouching by Juliette's mom's bed, both of them giving the camera a thumbs up while Tank has medicine and a surprisingly good-looking breakfast whipped up.

The favor he owed me was for saving his ass in the last skirmish with the Buzzsaws, so he owed me hard.

"How…?" she says, mouth agape.

"He told her an old friend of Diesel's wanted to give you some time off," I say simply. "That's technically not a lie. Looks like she's buying it. Tank will take care of her, and she has your own instructions to go on. I know it must sound funny coming from me, but you've got to trust me here."

She stares at me in disbelief for a few seconds, blinking slowly as she tries to wrap her head around her situation, still putting on as tough a face as she can muster despite how scared I can tell she is just under the surface. I've had a long time to know what fear looks like, and she might not be panicking, but I'm not out of the woods with her yet. Trust builds slowly--slower if you kidnap someone.

"Well, if you wanted to poison me, you wouldn't have gone through all the trouble of taking care of her," she half-mumbles ruefully as she glares daggers at me and attacks her food, shoving it into her mouth ravenously once she gets a taste for it.

I look away from her and run my hand over my shaved head so I'm not staring at her while she eats, but this isn't going well. I need to get her to see my point of view and that this is for the best. If scaring her into it is what needs to happen, so be it.

"Look, I know how this looks," I say plainly. "Neither of us are stupid. But you're somewhere safe and comfortable, and I have this place very well stocked with canned and dry food. Anyone could live here for weeks without trouble. But it's cold enough in the nights now that you do *not* want to try wandering out there on foot, so don't get any funny ideas. You won't reach town, not where we're at. You're safer here, anyway."

"You *kidnapped* me!" she says.

"For your *protection!*" I retort.

A tense silence hangs between us, and my heart is pounding just as fiercely as hers clearly is. It doesn't help that the way the light is hitting her still makes her look like a goddamn dark angel in the sheets, and it makes it all the more infuriating that I can't have what I want with her right now. Not like this.

"You weren't taking my warning seriously," I say, sitting back and letting my shoulders relax as she resumes eating. "You're in danger, and you need to know exactly how much danger you're in, and why I did this. The Buzzsaws hurt people, Juliette. They hurt women, treat them like property. They're *those* kinds of bikers. They've been using strip clubs up and down the state as bases of operation. When the girls don't comply, they get hurt--or worse. I've seen it."

She's listening to me with rapt attention, and by the way she's trying to keep her face from showing emotion, I can tell it's upsetting her. I wish I could avoid it, but some lessons have to hurt.

"That's why you're out here," I say. "Because you obviously won't stay out of the line of fire, so you're going to stay here until we can get this war settled."

"You mean you're keeping me here, because I'm your prisoner," she corrects me, narrowing her eyes, and I frown.

"You're the one who wants to use that word," I say, cracking a gruff smile. "Not me. But if you want to call it that, fine," I say, standing up--she doesn't flinch, nor does she break that defiant eye contact with me.

Fuck, I'm never going to get her out of my mind. I can just feel it.

"I don't need you to cooperate to keep you safe, I just need you to stay put," I say. "Eat up. I have some things to take care of," I say, making my way out the door and locking her in before she has time to respond.

My heart is pounding with as much desire for her as anger. That willful girl doesn't know what's best for her, and getting her to see things my way is proving harder than I thought. But I couldn't just wait around for her to be the next victim of the fighting.

Even if Diesel would never put his own sister through the kinds of things he does to other women, collateral damage has already happened, and the war has barely started. And with a growing gang like the Buzzsaws that draws the most ambitious bastards on this side of the country, there's no telling when the power structure could change. And that's never bloodless, not for anyone involved.

I spend the day taking care of sprucing up the so-called prison. I make sure all the electric is good and still working properly, set up some cameras around the perimeter to make sure I can keep an eye on her at all times, check in on Tank, and check all the locks on premise.

As I'm chopping firewood outside during the afternoon, I swear I feel the sensation of eyes on my back. My axe head crashes down on yet another piece of wood and splits it in half, but as I turn my head and let my gaze pan across the small clearing in the back of a long and winding dirt road where the cabin stands, it rests on the boarded-up bedroom window. There's a small enough gap between the boards that I bet a pair of eyes could watch through from within. I narrow mine at the window, and I wink. When I turn to go back to chopping wood, the feeling of being watched has passed.

Dinner is grilled cheeses with bacon and a hearty tomato basil soup--something simple, but filling and heavy. Once I've got it made, I take it back to the bedroom, carefully opening the door and watching for an attack from within. But when I step inside, I find that Juliette has fallen asleep, to my relief, and she seems to be a heavy sleeper. That, or she's pretending. Either way, I don't let my guard down as I carefully set the dinner down on the nightstand and take breakfast's dishes from her.

As I leave the bedroom and lock it behind me again, though, I hear a sound that makes my blood run cold: a motorcycle engine.

There shouldn't be anyone out here. *Fuck.*

I immediately have my hand on my pistol and start approaching the door before I get a look at the man riding the bike, bringing it to a halt in front of the cabin in the last beams of twilight through the trees.

"Breaker?" I grumble. "Tank, you motherfucking snitch."

Fifteen minutes later, I sit down on the couch opposite where the Heartbreakers' prez sits, taking his own dinner out of the fast food bag he brought with him, still glaring at me warily. I'm getting used to being alone in tense rooms with people, it seems.

"This is an act of war, Big Daddy," Breaker says.

"If keeping a civilian out of the fighting is an act of war, Prez," I say, holding my ground, "then that's the way it's got to be. I did what I know is right."

"There's going to be retribution for this, from the Buzzsaws," Breaker says. "This is a kidnapping, they won't take it lightly or give a fuck about your intentions."

"I know," I say. "And I'm prepared to deal with that. It doesn't change my mind about this."

"Little late to change your mind even if you wanted to, you are over that bridge my friend," he says with a gruff smile, then looking down.

"Don't you come at me with that," I say, sticking a finger out at him and making him raise his eyebrows--I don't normally tangle with Breaker, not like Bones does, but I care about the issue this time. "We're Heartbreakers. This whole club started when *you* pulled the same kind of stunt as this, remember? If you hadn't made a stupid-ass impulsive decision to save someone you thought didn't deserve getting hurt, we might not even be wearing these kuttes."

Breaker watches me for a few moments, then

chuckles softly. "You might be quiet, Big Daddy, but I know you've got a good head on your shoulders. No, I'm not going to come down on you too hard for this, but we need to figure out what to do from here."

"Besides kill Tank for snitching on me?" I ask, smiling.

"He did it for the good of the club--something you need to not lose sight of," Breaker says, something I've never been accused of before.

"That's why I brought her here," I say slowly. "To keep her *away* from club business. This is personal, or at least I consider it that way."

"Diesel won't," Breaker says, taking a deep breath...and then, a smile crosses his face that makes me wary. "Unless we put a spin on it."

"Huh?" I grunt. "What are you getting at?"

"We want to avoid war," Breaker says simply, leaning forward. "There are enough young riders in caskets out there. If there's any way we can keep the Buzzsaws out of commission without bloodshed, that's better than any alternatives."

"As long as we can bring the fuckers to justice, true enough," I say, nodding.

"We have lives at stake," he goes on. "Multiple kids are on the way in the club. They're going to be born into a warzone unless we can nip this in the bud. Now, we've been talking strategy and pinch points and supply lines until we've gotten blue in the face, but on the ride over here, I had an idea that might turn this into an opportunity."

"Hold on," I say, furrowing my brow. "I'm not about to let Juliette get used as some kind of bargaining chip."

Breaker's smile widens into a grin.

"Maybe not a bargaining chip," he says. "But how about a bride?"

My heart is beating like hummingbird wings. I can hardly believe the words I'm hearing. These guys are talking about me like I'm some kind of commodity. A bride? For whom?

Clearly, this is not a conversation I am meant to be privy to, but I managed to pick the lock in that admittedly cozy bedroom and sneak down the hall-way. I guess there are a couple things my big brother taught me. Lock-picking is among them. Obviously it took me a little time, first just to work up the courage to creep out of bed and across the room. I know better than to poke a bear. That's another thing I learned from Diesel. I don't get an especially threatening vibe from Big Daddy, but what do I know? He did just kidnap me. That's not a great indicator of his moral compass, probably. But then why did he help me? If he wants harm to come to me, he could have easily let that drunk guy catch up to me in the Muffler parking lot. He saved me and set me free. He let me leave. Only to capture me again! I can't make sense of it.

Once I finally convinced myself it was safe to try the lock, it took me a little while to work it open using a bobby pin I always keep tucked into my hair at the nape of my neck. While I picked the lock, I hardly dared to breathe. I sat totally silent, listening for any other sounds besides the shallow mechanics of my chest and the clicking of the lock. I worried that Big Daddy would hear me trying the door and come rushing to stop me. I don't get the sense he would really hurt me. In fact, if I'm totally honest with myself, everything feels calmer when he's nearby. It doesn't make any sense, but it's the truth. Still, whatever wires are crossed in my head to make me so drawn to my captor, I have to hold onto my goal: to get free. He may have found some guy to babysit my mom, but that's not good enough. And I don't like being told what to do.

Of course, I didn't expect to stumble upon this conversation between Big Daddy and one of his club brothers. I thought I could sneak out of the house and run away or at the very least get an idea of what the layout of the house is like. That way I can better plan a real escape. But now? I feel like all my plans have fallen apart in light of this new development. A wedding? They talk about it so casually, but to me, it's like a strike through my heart.

A storm of conflicting feelings overtake me. Apprehension. Panic. Confusion. And oddly enough, a strange lightning bolt of pure delight. I'm so surprised by that emotion it knocks me flat for a few moments. I have never given a lot of thought to marriage, or even dating. I've always had other priorities way ahead of it. So why is my heart melting? Why are my hands shaking? Why is there an annoying lump in my throat that won't go away?

No, I scold myself inwardly. That's weird. Don't feel that way. Stop it.

"You really got her locked up like a princess in a tower, huh?" the guy called Breaker says. I hold my breath, waiting for the answer.

Big Daddy grunts affirmatively. "Not my first choice of action, but I'm doing it to protect her. Even if she doesn't realize it yet. Or ever," he adds.

"Well, keep an eye on her. I have a feeling she's a runner," Breaker remarks.

"Yeah. You might be right about that," is the slightly amused response.

It dawns on me that this conversation might be drawing to a close any second now. I have to get moving before Big Daddy decides to come check on his captive princess. Careful not to take heavy steps, I softly pad down the hallway and slip back into the bedroom. I make sure to lock the door behind me, then I quickly flop myself back into bed, pulling the sheets up to my chin like a child hiding from a monster in the dark. I lie still for a moment, listening intently for any signs of my approaching captor. After a few minutes, I breathe a sigh of relief and decide I must have made my way back undetected. Now that I have a better idea of the blueprint, not to mention the startling news that I might become some biker guy's truce bride, I can start plotting my escape. I have to admit that so far, Big Daddy has treated me well. He's made accommodations for me and gone out of his way for me on a regular enough basis lately that I feel like he might be a decent person. You know, despite kidnapping me and all that.

But that other guy? I don't know about him. And if he's representative of the rest of the club members, I don't think I am totally safe here. I sit tangled up in the sheets for a long time, just picking through different escape scenarios in my mind. I sit and I listen. To my annoyance, the guy called Breaker ends up hanging around longer than I expect. As it turns out, my captor must be a surprisingly excellent conversationalist or something. They chat and skulk around the property for a while, and they're always just far enough out of earshot for me to not understand what they're talking about. Which, of course, is on purpose. I think. Probably.

I'm not sure what to think of Big Daddy. On the

one hand, he's kept me safe. On the other hand, he's caged me like a bird. And I told myself a long time ago I would never let that happen again. I have to be free. I just have to. But I know patience is key here. I can't rush my escape. Big Daddy isn't just brawn. He's got brains, too, and I won't be able to wiggle out from his grasp so easily. So I wait. And wait. And wait. I feel like I might lose my mind waiting. And then finally, I hear the distinct sounds of Breaker revving his motorcycle, coinciding with the footsteps of my captor coming up the hall. I freeze up, expecting him to come in and check on me. But he doesn't. I wait for it-- but the check-in never comes. At long last, I start to think the coast might actually be clear.

I have a plan. Not the best plan I've ever hatched, but the best I can think of. It will be an adventure and definitely a risk. Oh well. My freedom is worth it to me, I assure myself. It's worth it. I can do this. I wait for the right moment to arrive, and when I hear his heavy footsteps come into the room, I pretend to be asleep. I'm pretty good at that. Used to fake my mom into thinking I was asleep when she checked on me as a kid growing up, just so I could then flick on the lamp and keep reading late into the night. I utilize that superpower right now, and I'm pleased to find it effective. With one eye just ever so slightly parted to let shadows pass over, I watch Big Daddy stalk through the bedroom to the en suite bathroom.

He hovers in the doorway for a few moments just watching me. His eyes chart the soft, rhythmic rise and fall of my chest. I stay as still as possible, indicating a deep sleep. Once he's satisfied that I'm not going to jump up and run away, he closes the bathroom door behind him.

My heart is pounding. I know I only have a limited window in which to enact my plan. No room for mistakes. No time for hesitation, either.

I softly creep out of bed and sneak to the door. Listening closely, I start to open the bedroom door in tiny fractions, bit by bit until finally it was just barely open enough for my lithe body to slip through. Once I'm standing in the hallway, I listen again. Nothing. My dark hair whips out behind me as I dart down the hall to the front door. Every muscle in my body is tensed, every thought in my mind is screaming, pointing toward the door, toward freedom. But I stop at the door for a moment to do the thing I've been meaning to do, the thing I have been fixated on since I first caught a glimmer of the gold-tinted metal on the end table by the door.

The keys to the motorcycle. I grab them and hurriedly fumble to open the front door, struggling with my hands as they shake uncontrollably. I beg my body to calm down just enough to let me out. I take a deep breath, not daring to look back as I disengage three separate locks and burst out the door. I all but stumble down the driveway, my feet aching because I hit the ground so hard. I see the motorcycle. It's almost within grasp.

I scramble up to it, hoping my adrenaline will be enough to guide my shaking hands. Have I ever driven a motorcycle before? Nope. Do I have any clue where I am right now and which way to go? Not the foggiest. But will any of those negative little factoids change my mind now that it's made up?

Not at all. I'm fully committed.

Except maybe I'm not, I realize as I finally cast a glance back toward the house. I feel my heart lurch toward it, like it's longing to get back inside. Like I've left something totally vital behind and I need to go back for it. Guilt, I recognize, rearing its ugly head. Why do I get the sense that I'm not escaping Big Daddy, but betraying him? Abandoning him? Maybe it's the deep instinct within me that says he isn't a threat, that he's just trying to help. That he's got a heart of gold and the brightest intentions. Under normal circumstances, I would love to meet a guy like him. Smart, powerful, protective, thought-ful-- the strong, silent type I adore so much.

I try to shake off these feelings as I jam the key into the ignition. Or rather, try to. It seems like the adrenaline is too intense, because I can't aim the key into the hole properly. I try again and manage to catch it, but just before I can turn the engine, I feel a heavy hand weighing on my shoulder, and then a low growling voice in my ear.

"Nice try," Big Daddy grumbles, his hands grabbing me in mid-mount.

"Shit!" I yelp. For a moment I try to fight back, but I realize immediately that resistance is futile when it comes to Big Daddy. He's got a vice grip on me and I'm not going anywhere. So instead, I fix him with the most withering glare I can manage.

"Alright. Okay," he sighs, and promptly scoops me up into his arms.

"Hey! What are you-- put me down!" I retort indignantly.

"Chill out," he growls, carrying me up the drive and into the house. So much for my escape plan. He caught me like it was nothing, like he expected it.

"Just let me go," I protest.

"Tell me, where did you plan on driving that bike?" he asks.

"Away from here," I snap.

He chuckles. "In which direction?"

"Does it matter?" I splutter.

"If you want to continue being alive, yes. It matters a lot," Daddy answers.

"And you're telling me I'm safer here? With you?" I ask.

"Yes, I'm telling you that," he says emphatically. "The question is whether or not you'll listen to me."

"That depends what your intentions are," I groan.

He pauses for a moment as he carries me back

into the bedroom, confiscating the keys from me and tossing them on the dresser.

"Can you honestly look me in the eye and tell me you see bad intentions there?" he murmurs to me softly.

I try to meet his gaze, but it's too much. I avert my eyes.

"That's what I thought," he says, carrying me to the bed.

"So what are you going to do with me now?" I ask, afraid of the answer.

He cradles me back onto the bed and I hardly have a second to register what's going on before there are cuffs coming out and being pinned over my wrists, binding me to the bed.

"Wait. Wait! What are you doing?" I blurt out.

"Clearly, you're a high-risk prisoner," he says as he straps me in.

"Hey! I thought you said I wasn't a prisoner!" I whimper.

"And you said you are," he replies. "Just using your own terminology, little girl. Anyway, you've proven you can't be trusted. You require extra security. You're a flight risk."

"Extra security?" I squeak.

"Yes," he says. He steps back, folding his muscular arms over his chest. "I'm going to watch you all night."

I swallow hard. Nervousness swells up inside of

me. I don't like being watched. Or at least... I thought I didn't. But the strangest thing happens as Big Daddy stands guard in the room. Slowly but surely, my body starts to relax. Those tense muscles loosen up. My heart stops racing. My eyelids start drooping. I feel... safe. Of course, it takes a little wiggling to get comfortable being cuffed to a bed, but there's a quiet, insistent part of me that kind of loves it. And gets off on it. As I drift off to sleep, I can't resist the delicious fantasies that dance and whirl through my mind. My dreams are comfortable and blissful. Somehow, I get the best night of sleep I have had in what feels like forever.

When I wake up in the morning, it's to the tempting aroma of bacon sizzling through the chill air. I shiver a little as I come to life, my eyes taking in my strange surroundings. Although I'm slightly confused when I first wake up, it doesn't take me long to adjust. All the wild events of the past couple days come rushing back to me. I lie there totally still, staring up at the ceiling. Although my wrists ache a little, I feel totally rested. I don't even feel the need to struggle, and before long I'm joined by Big Daddy. He comes walking into the room with a tray of breakfast. My stomach growls loudly, betraying how ravenous I am.

"Morning," he said.

"Breakfast in bed? That's an odd choice to follow being handcuffed to the bed," I remark.

He sets the tray down on the bedside table and promptly unlocks my cuffs, to my surprise. He watches me quietly while I go through a truncated morning routine. He lets me go to the bathroom, wash my hands, even take a brief shower after I scarf down my breakfast. All the while, Big Daddy stands guard nearby.

"Tell me, do I need to keep you cuffed during the day or will you stay put?" he asks.

"I guess that depends," I admit slowly.

"On what?" he asks.

"On what I overheard between you and Breaker last night," I pipe up.

He looks amused, but not angry. Not even that surprised.

"I'm impressed. But if it makes you feel any better, I'm not comfortable with Breaker's… plot either," he tells me. "I'll explain it to you just the same."

"Please do. But first, do you have coffee?" I ask.

He smiles. "Yes. But you'll have to drink it black."

I nod. "Fine by me. I like it that way."

We sit and sip coffee out of oddly adorable mugs while he explains the plan. We are to set up a fake relationship in a big hurry, be seen together and witnessed in public, get married in a public place, and thereby halt the war before it can come to a head. Big Daddy reveals that my brother Diesel isn't willing to negotiate with them.

"But if his own sister is tied to the Heartbreakers, it might be enough to draw a truce. Save a few collateral lives, at least," he says.

I'm stunned. "That's not at all what I was expecting to hear," I confess.

"I know. It's a lot to take in," he concedes.

"It's just that he's my brother, you know? It's hard for me to picture him being that evil. But I can see him being involved in some violent stuff. He doesn't have the best group of friends these days. Maybe a peace agreement would help my family, too," I give in.

And maybe the way Big Daddy looks dazzling in the soft morning light is affecting my ability to make that call. Maybe the way my heart skips a beat every time he looks at me is obscuring my vision a little. But the plan sounds considerably less insane to me. I can see the potential benefits. Most importantly, I can feel that his intentions are clear. He wants peace. So do I.

"Don't worry," he says suddenly. "I told Breaker no."

"Oh," I mumble. "Okay."

"I'm still going to keep you here with me, but I'm not going to force you into anything formal. Not without your ready consent," Big Daddy assures me.

I'm oddly flattered that he would even take my feelings into consideration.

"I've been assigned to guard you, either way. It's technically personal rather than business, but it is what it is," he says.

"Okay," I mumble, nodding. "But I have something to ask of you."

He looks wary. "What is it?"

"Can you take me into town?" I ask.

Big Daddy frowns at me. "What?"

"I need to see my mom," I insist.

"No. Absolutely not," he replies. "Hell no. I'm sorry."

"Please, Daddy," I beg fervently. "She means the world to me, alright? My mom is the whole reason I moved back home to this dumb beautiful state and I need to know she's okay."

"Juliette…" he sighs.

"Come on," I insist. "Plus, you said yourself Breaker wants us to be seen together if we're going to set up our fake marriage, right?"

He looks at me hard, and I can tell he's thinking of how to answer me.

"That's your *condition*, I'm guessing," she says not even an hour later, when I'm standing in front of her holding up a simple, fresh black bandana, one that I've worn over my face more times than I can remember over the years.

"Yeah," I grunt. "I'm taking a risk letting you out of that *room*, much less the house. But knowing what I know about you, you're so liable to run anyway you're probably safest at my side anyway. Either way, you can't know where we are, so we're using the blindfold. Be lucky I'm not making you keep your hands bound."

She watches me suspiciously as I approach, but she at least doesn't stop me as I raise the blindfold to her eyes. Before the fabric can reach them, she snatches it from my hands and puts it on herself. I raise an eyebrow, smiling gruffly at her as I watch her tie it, and I give a single chuckle.

I take her by the hands and hold them up to her, not letting myself dwell too long on how warm and soft she feels under my rough grasp. "These are staying with me as long as we ride. You're not getting that thing off you until I'm ready to let you have it off, understand?"

"So," she says as I let go of her hands and step around her to the other side of the room to rummage through one of my bags. "You don't think the state troopers are going to think it's a little weird that you're riding around with a blindfolded woman on the back of your-"

Before she could finish her question, I gently slid a sleek black helmet over the top of her head and the blindfold. I opened the visor briefly to make sure the blindfold was still on, and I smiled at my handiwork when I shut it.

"Fair enough," she says. "But if you bust your head open and we die in a bike accident, I'll kill you."

"Deal," I grunt, and I take her by the hands and lead her out the door.

I have to admit, the circumstances are way too nice for me to be leading my kidnappee out the front door. The sky is clear and deep blue, the crisp October air outside makes me want to ride aimlessly for miles, and the girl I'm leading by the hands...well, it isn't a conventional first date, it's going to have to do.

I have no idea what the hell Breaker was thinking last night, tossing the marriage proposal into my court so casually like that. He must have known I'd be so stunned by that idea I could barely respond at the time. Marrying Juliette? Fuck me, I'd be a liar if I said the thought of how she might look in a black bridal dress didn't make my blood run hot, but I don't think I exactly tick the boxes for husband material.

I'm the enforcer for a motorcycle club. We've got a job to do. *I've* got a job to do, and faking a romance isn't in my job description.

But damned if Breaker doesn't have a point, too. The girl I help into her seat after we cross the yard and reach the glistening black behemoth of a motorcycle I ride is the sister of someone very important. She's valuable to the club. That's hard to argue. But shit, I hate thinking of her that way. She's a human being, not a pawn in a gang war.

I took her to keep her safe, not to use her against our enemy. But then again, that just makes Breaker's plan seem to make all the more sense. If it looked like Juliette and I were really together and had something going, and we happened to get hitched to seal the deal, it might stop the war before it even gets off the ground. If the war stops before it starts, that's as safe as it can possibly be for her, right?

Hell, maybe even she can sense that. I know she was joking earlier, but is it me, or does she not hate the idea as much as I'd expect? Maybe she's even more pragmatic than I am about all this, but marriage isn't something I've ever taken lightly. I don't know if I ever plan to tie the knot, but I wouldn't consider something like this unless...well shit, this is about as "do or die" of a situation as you can get, isn't it?

Once we're both on the bike, I hold her hands around my torso and against my stomach, where I hold them fast to me. "Alright, listen," I say. "We're going straight down to your mom's place, and when I say we can't be there more than a few minutes, I mean it."

She nods, and I feel the helmet bump against the back of my shoulders. I pause.

"Can you breathe okay?" I ask.

Another bump.

"Good. Might not be our only stop, either, so hang tight," I say as I fire up the engine, and the motorcycle roars to life under us.

I feel her hands tighten, then relax as the rumble makes its way through our bodies, and I smile down at her hands briefly before I pull off. She must not have ridden much, which is surprising, considering who she is. I kind of like that about her. She's new to this, and at the very least, that means I get to give her that first experience.

To my surprise, she's not as tense as I thought she'd be as I weave my way out the driveway and down the winding dirt path to the main road, where we empty out onto a broad, empty highway the likes of which keep me going more than anything else in the world. The road means freedom, and I get my strength there.

The softly rolling forested green hills all around us are overgrown with vibrant colors and tall, healthy trees that loom around us as I ride through the hills, smelling the fresh water in the air and the rich earth all around. I wonder if she's smart enough to figure out where we are based on senses alone, when we get back to the drier air and more open spaces back in Wyoming. I don't doubt she can, if she tries. She's impressing me at every turn, and I hate that I can't let her know that.

I don't pull over onto the side of the road until we're well into Wyoming, heading directly south toward Juliette's hometown. My eyes are watchful for any signs of other riders, but the roads seem to be quiet today, which I'm grateful for. Juliette deserves a breather. She's been through a lot in the...how long has she known me? Not even a week.

It's been a hell of a reunion.

The dark brown locks shake free from the helmet, and I pull the blindfold off her swiftly. Her eyes spring open immediately, then shut tight again and turn with her whole head as the sun stings her.

"Ow," she says plaintively.

"Yeah, welcome back to big sky country," I chuckle. "Feeling alright? Need to stretch your legs a little?"

"Nah, I'm good," she says, shaking her head and rolling her shoulders back, though she doesn't sound especially convincing. "Let's keep going."

"You've got a lot of energy," I point out as she gets back onto the bike with my help. "Sure you've never ridden before?"

"I got places to be," she says matter-of-factly. "Kidnapping or no, I'm getting down there."

She promptly wraps her arms around my torso just like they'd been before, and I raise an eyebrow at her in my mirror before giving a slow nod.

"Alright, trooper," I grunt. "If you insist."

We head off again, and this time, I don't even bother putting her hands in mine. I trust her not to jump off the bike, and she at least proved that she wants to prove that she can handle my trust, that much is clear. She knows she can get what she wants from me as long as she plays ball. If that means she's cooperating instead of fighting me every step, I won't complain.

When we finally reach the address, I have to say, it looks cuter in person than I expected. It's a simple but tidy, boxy house in a quaint suburb where I doubt they get so much as a noise complaint here.

As expected, Tank is waiting for us at the

window when we pull up, and he has the door open for us as I lead Juliette to it, not letting her off my hand. I'm not trusting her *that* much.

"Hey hey, good or bad timing, depending," Tank says as he steps into the doorway, pointedly standing in front of it before Juliette can try to rush past him. "Pam's asleep. She felt cozy after the brunch I fixed up, so she's snoozing in the armchair."

"Oh thank god," Juliette breaths, but she doesn't look relieved yet. "Can I see her?"

Tank looks to me, and I nod, so he steps aside and lets me lead her in. She makes her way to the entry of the living room and sticks her head in, with me right behind her.

Juliette's mom is sleeping soundly on the sofa, the remnants of brunch, and a half-empty glass of water on the table beside her. There's a peaceful and satisfied look on her face as her chest rises and falls, and Juliette watches her closely for a few moments, her eyes attentive.

Finally, I see her take a deep breath after Pam stirs in her sleep, and Juliette closes her eyes for a moment, tension washing away briefly before she looks back up at me and nods, swallowing. The three of us step back outside, and Tank leans on the doorframe after closing the door behind us.

"Wait," she says, eyes suddenly going wide. "I know why that was too quiet. Where's the dog?"

Tank quietly points up to one of the windows,

where a little dog is standing up on its hind legs, staring intently at the lot of us downstairs.

"In time out on Pam's orders, but I told her to go easy. We may or may not get along alright. I'm a dog person, what can I say?" Tank says with a shrug of his shoulders.

Juliette takes a deep breath, then looks up to me, not with a smile, but with a hard, searching gaze. "Thank you," she says at last, letting her face soften. "I don't know what I was expecting from all this, but you're...doing a hell of a lot more than I'd expect any ordinary kidnapper to do, I have to admit," she says, cracking a smile.

"And I wouldn't be doing any of it if I didn't think there was a real chance you could get hurt," I say, nodding slowly. "And we're not out of the woods yet, so get back on the bike."

"Drive safe, you two," Tank says sarcastically, waggling his fingers after us.

"And thank you too," she says as she follows me to the bike, but her tone is more warning than anything. "But you take good care of her, you hear me? If my mom complains *once*, I'll hear about it, and I'm coming for you."

"Jesus, Big Daddy, sure she's the one who got kidnapped?" Tank says, grinning at Juliette as she gets on the bike behind me.

"Oh she's mine alright," I growl, oddly proud of her. "If you can't handle her, that's your problem."

My engine roars, and we speed off down the road with Juliette's arms wrapped tight around me. To my surprise, I feel her closer than before--her whole body hugs me as I steer us toward the highway, and my heart starts to race as my cock starts to swell between my legs. She's not just hanging on, she's holding, and the difference feels like night and day.

Juliette sticks up for the people she cares about with a sharp tongue, and I've gotta say, it's kind of hot to see her use it. She didn't take shit from Diesel the day we met, and she's only gotten better at it over the years, by the sounds of it.

There are so many ways I want to get to know her, and none of the opportunity. But maybe we did have some kind of opportunity ahead of us, now that I thought about it.

"I'm taking a detour," I shout back at as I take a different exit to head northward. "We're stopping by the clubhouse on the way back."

"The what?" she asks.

"It's our base of operations," I say. "More importantly, it's got a bar. I'm buying you a drink."

She doesn't reply with words, but after a few seconds of contemplative silence, I feel her get more comfortable back there, and the rest of the road to Pine Haven feels so much more relaxed than the drive down that I can almost forget we aren't out on a date.

When I step through the bar to the downstairs

clubhouse, I'm grateful to see that none of the senior members of the club are around right now. The clubhouse has the kind of biker look and smell that anyone could recognize from a mile away, but the downstairs has a special sort of speakeasy vibe that I'd never admit I've always wanted to show off to someone special. The clubhouse was a special place for me, and I couldn't think of a better way to be seen with her for the first time.

There were plenty of prospects around, after all, and gossip spread fast.

"Are you...someone important in this club?" she asks with growing surprise as she looks around us.

"Hn?" I grunt, following her gaze, and then I notice what she's seeing. There are pictures of the core four of us--Breaker, Bones, Ironside, and me-- all over the damn place. And then there's my name, listed under the officers, and the word ENFORCER is emblazoned next to it.

"Oh," I say. "Nah. I just do my job."

"And what's an enforcer's job?" she asks, looking up at me with the kind of curiosity that tells me she knows it probably isn't pretty.

"I enforce," I decide to say simply as we reach the bar, and the bartender is already making his way over to us. I look to Juliette, then crack a smile. "Remember what you got last time you were here?" I ask.

"Gin and tonic," she says, rolling her eyes with a

smile. "It was nasty, I don't know why I thought I'd like it. But the second drink was a rum and cola, and I liked that."

"Thought you might," I say, and the bartender is already making it before I have to nod to him.

Juliette notices the fact that the prospects around the clubhouse tend to give us some privacy, or as some might have called it, a wide berth.

"Are people like me usually not down here or something?" she whispers to me as the bartender sets her drink in front of her and my usual straight bourbon in front of me.

"You mean women or civilians?" I grunt. "Because we got plenty of both. We're not what you'd call traditional. Breaker's girl is who designed this whole place down here."

"You're kidding," she says, genuinely in disbelief.

"What, did you think I was making up everything I told you about what kind of bikers we are?" I ask.

"Yeah-huh," she says bluntly.

We stare at each other for a few silent moments, then I can't hold the smile off my face any longer, and we let ourselves laugh quietly and turn to our drinks while she tries to keep me from noticing the blush in her cheeks.

"Thanks for the drink," she says, more sincerely. "Again."

"Hope it's a better experience than last time," I say, raising my glass to hers.

"I'll drink to that with my own kidnapper, sure," she says matter of factly, and she clinks her glass to mine.

After we take a long drink, she sets hers back down and looks to me earnestly. "So...you've got me behind enemy lines, a drink in my hand, and as far as I know, nobody knows I'm really gone yet," she says, swirling her drink around and looking up at me with remarkably calm defiance, despite how powerless she surely knows she is here. "Isn't this the part where you bring up the wedding again?"

"Looks like all I had to do was wait for you," I point out coolly.

"You know who my brother is, you don't think I'm used to bikers dishing out orders at me?" she says, smirking with bravado that I can't help but admire. "I just want to know what to expect."

"Those are the words of someone who's used to handling some real shit," I observe.

She waves it off as if I hadn't said a thing. "The whole reason I'm down here is to handle some real shit. And apparently, I just can't seem to do that, either," she goes on with a self-deprecating laugh that makes me frown. "That was the most peaceful that house has been since I pulled up. Figures, maybe me getting kidnapped was better for Mom after all."

"You didn't know you were stepping into a warzone," I say firmly. "You can't blame yourself for wanting to help your mom."

"I just picked a bad time to start," she says, raising her eyebrows. "I can only worry so much on each relative, you know."

There it is, I think to myself as the bartender brings our second round. That's why the idea of the wedding isn't a total brick wall for her. She's seen the club, she knows we may well be the people we say we are--and *I'm* at the very least legitimate.

She's starting to come around to the fact that a wedding might really be a solid option to stop the war.

"Well, since *you* mentioned it," I say with a teasing smile. "What would your ideal wedding look like?"

She blinks, then nearly spits her drink out laughing. "Tied up on the back of a motorcycle getting taken to Nowhere, Wyoming, and having a honeymoon in a creepy cabin in the woods, obviously."

"Careful joking like that," I growl through a smile. "We can make that happen all too easy."

She looks like she wants to throw a comeback at me, but something makes her regard me thoughtfully before tucking a loose lock of hair behind her ear and tilting her head to the side.

"So you really are serious? You think this could keep my brother out of trouble?" she asks, hiding how she feels about that thought very well in the tone of her voice.

"I don't know," I admit. "All I can do is hope. He's your brother, and if there's one thing bikers respect, it's bonds. We're tight like this because we're families, us MCs. Breaker, Tank, they're people I've learned to look at like my own brothers. I grew up in an orphanage, so family's one thing I'll always *make*, and I look out for family."

I say it all without much ceremony, because they're all simple facts. But Juliette watches me the entire time with a thoughtful, almost puzzled look on her face.

"You're doing better than me, so I can admire that," she says with a smile, and I return it.

"There's another reason Breaker might be interested in this wedding, too," I say. "I won't lie to you. A while ago one of our guys, Bones, fought this asshole named Brandon who tried to put something in a girl's drink. That girl's name is Lauren, and they're together now, but that's another story. Brandon's a veteran with a senator dad, and they're giving the town hell for it--and that hurts us."

"And a wedding would help your image," she says, raising an eyebrow.

"Bingo."

She doesn't look at me the same way she did when we left this morning. She's looking at me like someone who has something to bring to the table for her in the same way she can solve a lot of problems for our club. And that's the kind of person who will bargain.

"Think it over on the ride home," I say, tossing back the rest of my drink. "That's all I'll say for now."

As I lead her up and out of the bar, there are eyes on us, and they're both amused and interested. I have a reputation as someone who says little and does my talking with my hands. I'm not the type to open up like I did back there. Shit, I don't even know what got into me. I can't shake the feeling like I've been waiting longer than it feels like to talk to her, and I've never felt that before.

"Hey," she says, stopping me as we reach the porch and start to head to the parking lot. "By the way...thanks for not throwing me under the bus with your friend Tank earlier. I wasn't expecting backup, I was just giving him a hard time."

I smile, and maybe it's the buzz I'm still feeling from the conversation more than any booze, which hasn't touched me in the slightest, but the desire I've been feeling for Juliette building up in our time together reaches a peak as I see her under the pale sunset light.

"As long as you're with me," I say, "you can mouth off to anyone you goddamn like, girl."

"Even you?" she asks with a challenging smile, and I meet it, taking a step forward that almost takes her by surprise--almost.

"You want to find out?" I growl, reaching around to run my fingers into her hair. She doesn't stop me as I wrap it around my fingers and curl it into a fist.

Her cheeks blush a bright red as I tilt her head back, and I press a kiss to her lips.

My heart thuds heavily as I push her back into the lamppost and hold her against me while her hands grasp my kutte. She doesn't just return my kiss, she leans into it with a fiery energy that feels every bit as *pissed off* as it is turned on. I can't help but smile into the kiss, and that just pisses her off more.

Fuck, she must have been more wound up than I thought. Not like she did a good job of hiding it. I gripped her ass and pulled it toward me, grinding our hips together, and I felt the warmth of her body against my own hardness. She moved as if she was electrified, desperate to feel me as my tongue brushed against hers, and we melted into making out shamelessly under the setting sun.

People saw. We were conspicuous. It was perfect. And we didn't have to do a scrap of acting to make it happen. If this was how her body was reacting, then I was going to strike while the iron was hot.

"Let's get you home," I growl. "I'm starting to think you like getting yanked around like this."

"Fuck you," she hisses, and I take her back to the bike.

The ride home under the moonlight is a dream, and she doesn't even object when I have to slip the blindfold back over her eyes.

After getting home, my heart is still pounding as

I lead her inside and let her get ready for bed. As she climbs into the sheets and sees that I'm holding the handcuffs again, ready to restrain her to the bed to make sure she doesn't pull another stunt like the motorcycle incident, she bites her lip.

"It's got to happen, girl," I growl, even though I've got a smile on my face.

"I...I know," she says. "But aren't you cold at night?"

"Huh?" I grunt.

"I'm freezing under these sheets," she says, bunching them up as she curls her legs under them. "And I hate that you just have to deal with the couch."

I want to tease her, but what I hear under her words is unmistakable, and it touches my heart in a way I am not expecting. I run a hand over my head as I stand up and slip my kutte off as she looks up at me with glimmering dark eyes.

Wordlessly, I kneel down in the bed beside her, and although I'm ready to lay on my back away from her, she immediately curls into me, pushing her butt against my thigh and shivering. I can't bring myself to do anything but wrap my arms around her, and I reach up to the bedpost and click the handcuffs onto her.

She swallows, looking up at it and then back down to me. I realize that I can feel her heart pounding under my hands, and I realize just how aware she is of the fact that I've got her more than helpless here. She's not a girl who's used to not having control in a situation, or at least being able to strive for it. I can feel so much goddamn tension in her back that it makes *me* ache. I'd almost dare say she likes the feeling of me holding her so vulnerably like this.

I'm a quiet man, but I'm not stupid. I've gotten to know Juliette enough to see why the thought of giving up a little control might be...appealing, in a special way. If that's how she feels, then it's only my duty to oblige.

"Do you know what you're asking for, girl?" I growl, slowly sliding my hands up her side, slow enough for her to stop me if she truly wants.

"Yes," she whispers, a syllable that makes my cock twitch and swell.

"Do you want it?" I say in a rumbling, low voice. "Do you want me to help you relax, Juliette? I can feel what's good for you. I've been feeling it all damn day."

"Show me, Daddy," she says in a soft, almost begging voice, ashamed of herself for uttering it.

I'm going to reward her for it.

I slide my hand down between her legs and under the fabric of her underwear while my other goes up her shirt. She doesn't stop me.

"Safe word," I growl.

"Burger," she whispers.

"Hungry?" I grunt curiously as my hand cups her breast.

"Fuck you," she hisses, and I grin as I touch her clit. "*Oh!*"

The gasp is music to my ears as I slowly start to circle two fingers around what I find to be a wet pussy. I slide the tips of my fingers further into her, then draw them back out and bring them to my lips before I press a kiss to her neck. I can hear her panting breathing quick and hot, and her nipple is stiff under my thumb.

My cock is hard as a rock, too, and the blood pounding through my massive frame wants nothing more than to claim the girl who's been haunting my dreams for years. But tonight, she just needs help sleeping, and I want to make her feel the kind of relaxation I've wanted to bring her for so long.

I concentrate on swirling my fingers around on the swollen button of her clit, and I feel her writhe against me with a mouth hanging open. Her breathing becomes a heavy panting, and she bites her lip and whimpers, a sound that wrenches my heart and makes it even harder not to tear the sheets off and let her feel what she's doing to me.

Instead, I channel that hunger into tormenting that poor clit.

As I feel her getting closer to her orgasm, I slow down, change the rhythm, and get her to start over again. She can feel me doing it, and I love those frustrated little groans when she realizes that I'm tormenting her.

But there's no escape.

I drag my little game out as long as I please, all the while feeling up her breasts and grinding against her ass. We say nothing. We don't need to.

"Fuck," she hisses as I keep the tempo steady, building her up slowly and steadily, feeling the natural desires of her body in the way she moves when I touch her. I'm done winding her up, it's time to put her to bed.

She grabs bunches of the sheets in her fist and buries her face in the pillow as she cries out with the sudden orgasm in the cool, dark cabin room. I hold her tight and guide her through it with a steady stroking pace, chuckling softly as I feel the slick honey on my fingers, hot and wet.

"Just doing my duty," I growl, pecking her on the cheek. "As a fiancée."

She gives an exhausted murmur that sounds almost like a thank-you, but Juliette is spent. And as she drifts off into a peaceful sleep, I'm left to sit in sleepless silence with a sore tightness between my legs.

JULIETTE

I'm drifting along down a quietly babbling creek with crystal-clear waters and tall white trees looming like ancient guardians on either bank. Dark green moss grows thickly across the smooth faces of stones, and teeny-tiny fishes with glittering silver scales dart here and there, disappearing as mirages in the shine of the current. I feel totally weightless. My body is a feather at the soft mercy of the water, whirling in the pools and collecting at the tips of waterfalls. Every motion is gentle. The forest surrounding me breathes and thrums with life of every kind. Black and orange butterfly wings beat alongside tiny hummingbirds, sharing rather than competing around the fluffy center of a flower. I watch them alight on the petals opposite one another, and not even the faintest hint of a struggle ensues. They dip down in alternating motions, one takes, and then the other. I'm entranced by the come and go of their little pollination dance, so distracted that I feel my eyes starting to flutter. Like softly beating wings. Like a curled baby leaf, trembling bright green under the gift of dew. Although the water is cool, I feel totally warm from my head to my toes. All is calm. All is peaceful. All is well.

Someone is looking out for me. I know that wherever I am, I'm safe. No one can reach me here. I'm cocooned in the radiant arms of what feels like real, genuine affection. And when my eyes do finally open in the hazy light of dawn, it doesn't take long to figure out why I'm feeling that way. Even though the ache in my wrists tells me I'm still cuffed to the bed, the rest of my body feels perfectly comfortable. I'm cradled gently and protectively in the arms of my handsome captor. I can feel the hardness of his muscular body pressed against my side, his breath rolling across my head. He holds me close, like I'm something precious he doesn't want to lose. Like if he were to let go of me I would float away. Lately, it has felt a little bit like I'm in a fantasy land. Not that it's been all pleasant, but this part? This quiet intimacy with Daddy? I can't help but enjoy it. I love to be kept safe in his embrace. I know nothing can touch me as long as he's around to watch over me.

And yet, I can't seem to shake that little tingle of guilt at the back of my mind. As comfortable as I am, thoughts about my family come sneaking back in. Diesel may not be the shining example of goodness one would want in an older brother, but he's still my blood. Surely that has to count for something. If it doesn't, then what have I come back here for? I returned to help my mother through a medical crisis, as a good daughter should. Or so I thought. But if I can so brazenly defy my brother, does that invalidate all the help I've tried to give my mom? Can I be both ally to her and enemy to him at the same time? I wish things could be that simple. Black and white, clear lines. But it seems like the longer I spend in this state, the blurrier the lines become. It all smudges together, more watercolor than acrylic. Big Daddy makes me second-guess all the assumptions and self-truths I have been carrying all these years. I can't pretend like there isn't a big part of who still feels abandoned, deep down. After all, I lost my father when I was young, and then I slowly lost my brother to his sketchy, grimy friends. I lost him to the highway, to the rev and rumble of a motorbike engine. I lost him to freedom and the open road. I know it's not my father's fault he had to pass away, and with how unstable and temporarily depressing it was to be at home after his death, I kind of understand why Diesel would strike out to find some new distraction out of the house. He couldn't stay and wallow in the bitterness. Besides, Diesel has always been exceptionally good at keeping his own private store of bitterness. He doesn't need to add to the pile. And maybe I'm more like him than I ever thought, because I realize now that I've been carrying a lot of guilt and shame and pushed-down anger. I know it's not like I was intentionally abandoned, and yet it still feels that way sometimes. My childhood memories are studded with little jewels of sparkling pain, and I can't look back without wincing a little. But here, in the arms of my handsome captor, I can feel that pain, that bitterness, quaking at the edges around us, unable to penetrate the fortress of Big Daddy's embrace and reach me anymore. I'm safe, at least for the moment. I almost wish he would stay asleep for a few hours more, give me more time to lie pressed up against his hard body, protected and warm.

I have to quietly remind myself that I can't put all my eggs in one basket here, though. Everything about my dynamic with Big Daddy is based on a shaky, foundationless lie: that we are together in an official capacity. That we know each other well enough to commit to a marriage of both convenience and strategy. I feel kind of like some hapless medieval princess being sold off in marriage to a stranger for the sake of some ill-fated truce. Of course, I hope this truce meets a better fate, but that all depends on our ability to make it look real while evading questions about how and when we met, how we ended up betrothed so seemingly out of nowhere. People will have questions. My mother especially. It's only fair.

After all, I would be skeptical of our "relationship" from an outside perspective, too. We are an undeniably weird couple. Gigantic, muscular, brooding Big Daddy and petite, lithe, little me. He looks like he could devour me whole, and to be honest, I'm kind of okay with that. Sure, he still has my wrists in those restraints, but I think I would be here whether or not I'm bound to the bed. Even if my arms were free, I don't think I would feel particularly compelled to leave. Where the hell would I even go? There is no place safer or more comfortable than right here in this bed, under the sheets, with Big Daddy curled around me like a protective shield. I almost don't even want him to wake up anytime soon just so I can work in as much cuddling as possible. Naturally it does strike me as kind of unusual just how much joy and comfort I can get from forced proximity to my captor, perhaps. I ought to pull back, resist a little harder. I don't want people thinking I'm some shrinking violet who doesn't have the balls or the self-respect to deny my captor what he wants. But in this case, we clearly want the same things. At least for now. We can agree on snuggling in the mega soft bed here. And honestly, for the moment, that's enough.

I wriggle closer to my captor and feel his heartbeat thumping slow and calm against my side. I get goosebumps from his skin touching mine, hot and hard. He's a machine of pure rippling muscle. I can sense the enormous power thrumming inside of him, just barely held back. I know he could so easily tear me apart. I'm just an unwitting fly caught in his spider's web. He has me perfectly wrapped up, bound by my wrists and getting wrapped up further and further into his clutches. He's sneaky like that, but I can't pretend like I'm not totally into it. There are a lot of reasons why I haven't tried very hard to fight him off. Truth be told, under any other circumstances and with anyone other than him, I would have almost certainly taken a bigger plunge to escape by now. I don't like being held down in place. I don't like having my wings clipped. I want to be free to fly as high and as far away as I so desire. And yet? Being close to Big Daddy quells that instinct to flee within me. Breathing in his warm, musky scent makes my body loosen up and relax. Feeling his rock hard muscles circled around me like a fortress makes me feel important. Precious. Vital to somebody. And when that somebody is a guy as impressive as Big Daddy, it's hard not to feel a little puffed up. He has good taste, I can tell. I may not be his usual fare, but there's no pretending we don't fit and lock in together like two pieces of machinery handcrafted to go together. This is the best place in the world. The safest little corner of the universe and it's all ours for the taking.

So, naturally, I'm a little heartbroken when I feel him slowly stir to life and yawn as his powerful limbs stretch out around me. I know waking up means leaving this bed, and I'm quite content where I am.

A shiver of delight rolls down my spine when I feel him lean in close and press a soft, warm kiss to my ticklish neck. I giggle and writhe around in his arms, both wanting more and wanting escape from the tickly sensation.

"Morning," he grunts against my hair.

I rock back against him. "Yes it is," I remark.

"How long have you been awake?" he asks in a low, gravelly voice.

Ugh, I've always found men's voices to be particularly sexy first thing in the morning when it's kind of hoarse and scratchy. Mmm. Delicious.

"Not long. Just been soaking up your warmth. You're like a space heater, you know," I tease. "Do you have just a perpetual low-grade fever or something?"

"I'm just a powerhouse for heat. Totally healthy. And all the better to hold you with," he growls, pulling me tight to his chest for a glorious moment.

My heart is already soaring, my body warming and molding to his powerful shape. But before I can really snuggle in as close as I want to, I'm dismayed to find him pulling away. I wish my wrists weren't restrained so that I could grab hold of him and keep him near. But as always, I am reminded that he is the one in control. I'm at his mercy entirely. He can come and go as he pleases, but I am bound to his will rather than mine.

I'm embarrassed to realize that I'm actually quite okay with that. I like knowing I'm in such capable hands. But as soon as he slides out of bed, he leaves me feeling cold and lonely. There's an ache in my heart that I know can only be assuaged by Daddy's magic touch. I stare at him intently, my lips shaping into a luscious pout. I know how cute I am. I fully intend to use it to my advantage. Two can play at this game.

"You're going to leave me handcuffed?" I speak up.

He gives me a smirk over his shoulder.

"You sure seemed to like it last night," he tosses back.

I blush deeply and pull at my restraints for emphasis. Ugh, bastard. And yet I'm still turned on? Who am I?

"Come on. That's different. It's morning now. I have some things I need to do," I admit sheepishly.

He nods and walks back to the bed, reaching for the cuffs. "Fair point. I won't leave you here to suffer. That would be cruel," he admits with an easy smile.

"Thank god," I mumble, rolling my eyes.

The breath catches in my throat as his fingertips brush against the slightly irritated, sensitive skin of my wrists. It's a weird sensation somewhere between a tickle and a burn, but he works swiftly, and the moment I hear the cuffs clink open, my tired arms flop down to my sides, bouncing ever so slightly on the mattress. For some reason, my floppy arms are so funny to me that I actually burst out laughing. The relief in my body from being released of my shackles was damn near euphoric. For a few blissful moments I lie flat on the bed, just grinning up at the ceiling fan. Until Daddy leans over me with a concerned expression, that is.

"You alright?" he grunts.

"Oh yeah. I'm great," I reply. "I would give you a thumbs up but my arms feel like gelatin right about now."

"Well, then, it's a good thing my arms are still in fighting condition," he says, scooping his arms underneath my flimsy body and hoisting me up against his chest.

"I'm not paralyzed, Daddy. I can walk," I giggle.

"I've already got you in my arms. No wiggling out of this," he teases right back.

"You going to watch me pee, too?" I quip.

"You're on your own for that. Unless you're afraid of toilet snakes or something," he jokes. I gape at him openly as he sets me down on my feet by the en suite door.

"Toilet...snakes. Did you really just utter that phrase to me?" I scoff.

"It's a joke, Juliette. They're not real," he assures me.

"Where's the joke? I can't find it," I retort.

"Alright," he grouses. He does a spinny motion with his fingers, then shoos me into the bathroom. "Take your pee. Take a shower, too, while you're at it."

"Wow. Rude," I mumble.

"You smell fine, but you'll feel better after a shower," he instructs sagely.

"Okay, I'll shower. Jeez. You know you're not my real Daddy, right?" I tease.

There's a twinge of a smile on his lips, but the spark in his eye gives it away completely. He gives me a look up and down and shakes his head.

"How can you look like an angel first thing in the morning like that?" he murmurs.

My heart stumbles over a beat. I nervously twirl a lock of my tangled hair around my finger and grimace at the state of it. I glance at the mirror and full-on blanch.

"I look like a gremlin," I groan.

He laughs. "I don't know how you see anything but gorgeousness in that reflection, but I'll leave you to it. I'll put your clothes on the bed. Meet me in the kitchen when you're ready."

"Ready for what?" I pipe up.

As he's closing the door, he replies, "You've got a lot to learn, little thing."

Before I can ask any further, he closes the door and walks out. I hear the bedroom door shut, too. His footsteps disappear and it dawns on me that he is putting a lot of trust in me. He's gone the opposite direction of the front door. I'm not locked in. Theoretically, I can just turn on the shower water for white noise, tiptoe out into the hallway, and make a measured bid for the door. But then again, I am reminded quite sorely, there looms the same problem as before. Where would I go? Who would help me? How could I escape when I don't know which way to run?

And besides...I don't want to leave. I know that fact in the deep beat of my heart. I want to stay, to be wherever he is. So I dutifully go through my morning routine, put on the comically oversized clothes left out for me, and trot out to the living room, my damp hair dangling loose and heavy around my shoulders.

He does a double take when I walk in the room, able to see me from his vantage point at the kitchen counter. He waves me over. I follow the scent of sizzling bacon and eggs, the tick-tick of a toaster oven, and most importantly, the slightly bitter aroma of black coffee. The two of us pile up our plates and sit in the living room to eat while Big Daddy explains to me all the different ways in which a young woman like me could feasibly defend herself against assailants. My stomach churns as he talks about this topic. I hope to never end up in such dire circumstances. I don't want to fight. I will if I have to, but I will resist it until I'm cornered.

"Do you really think I'm going to need to know this information?" I ask.

He shrugs. "I don't know. But I would rather have you well-informed and prepared for the worst than let you remain...helpless."

I bristled a little bit at that. "I never said I was helpless," I assert.

"I know that. You're strong. I knew that the moment I saw you. But these men, these *associates* of Diesel, they know how to hurt people in a way that is almost barbaric. They don't share the same regard and respect for life as we do," he explains gravely.

"You're talking about my brother, you know," I hiss.

"Well, then for the sake of this exercise, let's keep Diesel out of the picture. Think of it this way: you're a young woman who's been sucked into the middle of a war. There are bound to be victims. Collateral damage. I don't want you to become that collateral damage. I don't want you to be a victim, Juliette. I want to help you protect yourself, just for the hypothetical moment in which I might not be there to save you," Daddy goes on, and I find myself enchanted.

He really does just want to help me. And he proves it over the next hour or so, walking me through the various ways I can fight back or at the very least stun my attacker long enough to give me some breath of a chance to escape them. He teaches me to kick at the knees, knee the groin, bite the hands, push the eyes and head-butt the nose. He shows me step by step how to block someone's attack, how to tuck and roll away, how to swipe at my attacker's ankles and scream as loud as I can in his ear. That one was especially fun to learn.

Before long, we've worked our way down from standing, to crouching, to kneeling, to toppling over together on the floor of the living room. Almost wrestling, not quite laughing, but my heart is hammering a million miles a minute. Every brush of his firm body against mine lights a fire inside of me. It's almost hard to breathe, the desire is so thick. And I can tell that the feeling is mutual. His cock strains hard through the fabric of his pants as we roll and caress and explore one another's bodies. I tilt my head back as he roves down my body, kissing and clawing his way down. I tremble and twitch at every stimulating moment of friction, and I roll my hips upward to meet him, eagerly encouraging him to devour me. And devour me, he does.

His tongue goes rigid and circles my clit, waking me up with a few zaps of what feels like electrical pleasure. I buck and whimper under his hot, wet mouth, my folds getting slicker by the second. He plunges his tongue in and out of my aching cunny and darts back out to roll up and down my twitching petals. It's almost hard to remember to breathe, I'm so turned on. I just can't get enough of him. Every surface of his body, every movement of his mouth against my flesh, the soft growls and groans that escape his throat as he takes me for everything I am. He's masterful with that tongue, and when he slips a long, hooked finger inside my pulsing pussy, I immediately curl my toes and cry out. An orgasm stumbles through me, making me convulse with involuntary twitches and sighs. It feels so damn good. A rush of golden warmth tingles in every cell of my body and all the tension I've been holding just melts away.

"You needed that, didn't you?" Daddy murmurs in a raspy voice.

"Mhm," is all I can manage.

"But we can do better than that," he says, whipping out his cock and starting to rub the broad, swollen head in a circular motion around my aching hole.

"Oh, you're teasing me," I whimper, biting my lip.

"I'm not teasing," he growls. "Do you want more, little girl?"

I nod fervently. "Yes. Yes, please. Don't stop."

"You want me to fuck this sweet little pussy?" Daddy asks.

"More than anything," I breathe.

His hands wrench my thighs further apart as he

lifts my legs to hook them over his shoulders. I can hardly keep my heart from falling out my chest as he lines himself up, the engorged tip of his cock pressing ever so slightly against my hole until he pushes inside a little. I cry out and grasp for his arms to steady myself as he slides into me slowly but fully. I feel tears prickling in my eyes, my breaths coming quick and shallow. I feel enormous waves of pleasure through my whole being, but there's a tinge of slight pain from how absolutely huge Daddy is inside of me. And that edge of pain is what drives me to feel even sexier than ever. I can not only take the pain with the pleasure-- I revel in it. I love the way it feels to have his massive, glorious cock spearing my tight little cunny open. His thickness stretches me with every inch, and once he's fully sheathed inside of me, there are still a couple inches he can't even fit. But he certainly tries, and the resulting slam of force into my unsuspecting g-spot makes my pussy gush, with a sudden, bright, searing climax that has me seeing stars dancing in the air. I feel myself closing and convulsing around his thick cock, and he softly rocks back and forth while I come down from the overstimulated intensity of my orgasm. I arch my back and lean into him, his strong arms snaking underneath my ass to lift me slightly. This new angle proves to be quite literally explosive. With a few rapid thrusts, he hammers into my g-spot relentlessly. When he uses one of his arms to continue lifting me and the other wanders to grope my breast, then down to massage my dripping wet folds, all while pummeling me with his cock... well, I'm a goner.

"Oh my god. Oh my god. Daddy," I whimper, a genuine tear beading up in my eye.

"Come for me, sweetheart. Give Daddy all that honey," he growls.

His thumb traces a perfect circle over my little pink clit at just the right moment and I come again, dousing his cock in a startling rain of juices.

"Fuck yes," he groans through gritted teeth. "You're so wet for me."

"It feels-- so good--" I choke out. "I want to feel you. Hard."

"Harder?" he purrs against my ear.

I nod eagerly, clawing at his back. "Please. Please, fuck me hard."

To my dismay, he pulls back and slips out of my cunny, making me pout with disappointment. I look up at him sadly.

"What did I do?" I murmur.

"Get on your knees," he commands. "Face that wall. Show me that beautiful ass."

I do as I am told. I kneel down almost in a praying position, then lift my ass up in the air. I look back to see Big Daddy running his hands over my smooth, bouncy ass. He spreads my legs farther apart and grabs hold of my hips to keep me in place. I inhaled sharply as his cock slides into me with one swift, piercing movement. I cry out and shudder around him, but he manages to hold me up with ease. He rears back and slides into my cunny again. He picks up the pace and the force, and before long, he's railing into me so hard I can hardly keep upright. Tears burn in my eyes and a blissed-out smile plays on my lips as he pounds my pussy harder and faster. Every snap of his hips and wet smack of his balls against my ass nudges me closer and closer to another orgasm. Finally, just as I'm feeling Daddy tense up and tighten his grip on my hips, I come again, slicking his cock with my juice. Not an entire heartbeat later, I feel his massive shaft pump and pulsate inside of me, shooting me full of his precious, creamy seed. We collapse together on the floor, side by side looking up at the ceiling while we catch our breath.

"Damn," he growls.

"Indeed," I pant.

Before we can say anything else, we're interrupted by the annoying buzz of a cell phone on wood. With lightning-quick speed, Big Daddy sits up and snatches the phone off the coffee table, sliding the screen open. He instantly looks concerned. I sit up next to him.

"What is it?" I ask.

"Breaker. He says he's about to call--" he breaks

off as the screen lights up. It's a call from Breaker. He hastily answers. "Hello? Breaker?" Daddy says.

I watch as he stands up and paces across the room. I can't hear what's being said on the other end of the line, but I can by the look on Daddy's face that something isn't right. All the bliss and peace that had graced my body in the afterglow went skittering away in the dark.

BIG DADDY

I end the phone call with the push of a button in the bedroom a few minutes later, and my face is grim as I lower my phone, feeling Juliette's intense gaze on me.

"Was that…?" she asks.

"What it sounded like?" I say. "Yeah. You said you thought nobody missed you--you were wrong. Your brother just asked for a meeting, and he wants to talk about you."

Her face pales briefly, but she looks more surprised than anything. "Really? That soon?"

"We're at war, Juliette," I say. "Eyes and ears are everywhere. I'd be surprised if we went unseen the whole way down to your mom's place. Just so happens that's for the best, if we want to go along with this plan."

"I do," she affirms, smiling faintly yet nervously,

and my cock stays stiff the whole time I can see her naked body only half-covered by the sheets, draped over her curvy figure so nicely I want to dive onto her for the next round. "If you really think this could avoid war, then I'll do it."

"Save the 'I do's for the altar," I say with a wink that makes her roll her eyes, despite her blush.

I get back into bed with her, and I lean against the wall as she curls into my side without prompting. Her soft hands slide over my firm, tight abs and meet on my side as she wiggles close, and I wrap a large arm around her and pull the sheets up. My hand squeezes her hip, and the last shiver of the chill in the room gets driven away by our body heat together.

I've fucked my prisoner, the darker part of my mind tells me. She doesn't seem to see it that way, judging by the way her whole body seems relaxed in a way I've never seen before. She always has this tension in her shoulders that shows in the way she walks, but she might as well be a wet noodle draped over me now.

She feels safe, I realize, and that startles me. I'm the kind of guy people stay a distance from walking down the sidewalk. They see me in traffic, they move. I'm no showoff, it's even inconvenient. It's hard to buy a new pair of black goddamn jeans when the clerks keep nervously trying to avoid me. If anything though, Juliette seems to enjoy it even more this way. She can be prickly, but she's different around me. I thought it was just in my head at first, but now that I've seen her around other people, I can't not notice it.

We sit in silence for a few long minutes, and I spend half of it wondering what's on her mind. But I've always been a man who talks with his hands, so I slid my hand up to the back of her neck, and I start gently massaging her with thick knuckles and a warm hand.

"Oh my god," she murmurs, closing her eyes softly and turning her head, bringing a smile to my lips. "I didn't know how much I need that. All of it," she says softly, filling me with a warmth from within that I'm not used to.

"If I'm going to be your husband, I might as well play the part," I say in a low, rumbling voice.

"Is being handcuffed to the bed what you have in mind for your wife?" she says, tilting her head to the side with a playful smile.

"Might be," I growl ominously, working my fingers into her back and sliding my other hand between her thighs.

She gasps as I feel her warmth and our wetness, and I shamelessly invade her to caress her pussy and keep both hands busy on her. Her mouth hangs open, and for longer than I cared to keep track of, I held her there, kissing her neck and rubbing her gently as I tried to soothe her body and mind together.

"The weirdest thing is," she murmurs, breaking the spell of silence. "I can't remember the last time I felt like this. Even back home."

I don't reply with words. I only hug her closer to me, sliding my hand out of her pussy at last and feeling my cock twitch at the soft whimper she lets out.

"So..." she says once we've moved out of gentle aftercare and start to feel sleep catching up to us. "It's a good sign that Clint- Diesel, wants to meet with you, isn't it?"

"What makes you ask?" I say.

"You seem uneasy," she replies.

"I'm always uneasy," I say with a wink.

"I get that vibe," she says, nodding.

"I'm just a suspicious guy," I admit, shrugging my shoulders. "I probably always will be. It served me well in the past. And you know I've dealt with Diesel. Hell, you know *him*. I'm the right amount of cautious."

"Can't argue with that if I wanted to," she admits, yawning as she rubs her eyes.

And soon, sleep takes us both.

The next morning, I'm leaning on the doorframe of the bathroom while Juliette showers, looking up at the ceiling with my arms crossed as I listen to the sound of the water pouring over her body with a swelling cock, smiling to myself. I'm keeping an eye on her just because this is still technically a kidnapping, but I have a feeling she'd object more if I were to leave her alone.

"So, what's the plan?" she asks from behind the curtain.

"We're meeting around lunchtime at a pub in a neutral location, somewhere the influence of the MCs doesn't mean as much--Cheyenne. It'll be me and Breaker, and I imagine Diesel will have someone with him, if not more."

"Why am I not in there?" she asks.

"Number one, because I honestly don't know what to expect, and I want you to be safe until I can be sure he's not going to try anything stupid," I say. "Number two, he doesn't know you're coming. If he feels uneasy or senses too many surprises, it could turn ugly."

"But what if he needs to know I'm safe?" she asks.

"Pictures," I say.

"He's not going to believe I'm really with you willingly unless I'm there," she insists, sticking her head out of the curtain, and my heart skips a beat at the sight of her wet, dark hair curling down her shoulders, eyes bright and alert after getting up late. "You know that."

I frown. She's got a point.

"Figured you'd fight me on that," I grunt. "Compromise: you'll wait outside with Bones. If you're needed, we'll pull you in."

She narrows her eyes at me for a few moments, then nods. "Fine." She then looks me up and down, and she looks more hesitant for a moment.

"Something on your mind?" I ask as I step forward, raising an eyebrow.

"How are you feeling?" she asks. "About the meeting?"

"I'd rather be keeping an eye on you," I say in a low tone, showing a faint smile. "I won't lie, I don't trust Diesel. But it's worth a try. Anything for my wife," I say with a wink that makes her blush.

"You can't call me that until we do the vows," she points out with a smirk, then averts her eyes. "But I can tell you're tense."

I sense the undertone in her voice, and when her eyes meet mine again, I get her meaning. Wordlessly, I pull my shirt off, and her eyes light up, confirming my suspicions. I strip down and step into the shower with her, and almost immediately, I clutch her sides and press her against the cool tile.

She sinks down to her knees under me, slipping away inch by inch and looking at me with pleading eyes. My nostrils flare as I regard her lowering herself to my cock, and I give a single nod.

I run my hands through her hair as she looks to my bulging cock and its dark, purple crown, and she wraps a hand around it tentatively. She swallows as she gives it a few experimental strokes, somewhat intimidated by the weight of it. It doesn't take her long to relax, though, and she brings her lips to the base of my trunk and presses a warm kiss to it.

As the hot water rolls over streams and channels of my muscles, I feel my crotch growing warm and delighted, and my heavy balls remind me how sore they are and needy for release. I've come inside her just last night, and they're already aching for more.

She wanders up to the tip of my cock and opens her mouth to give it a single long, firm lick before wrapping her lips around it. She moans softly as she takes more of it in, and as her tongue brushes over the slit of my cock, I let out a groan and let my head tilt back while the blissful feeling rolls up the length of my shaft and through every muscle in my groin.

She slides further onto me, and her tongue feels like heaven. I'm not the world's most poetic man, but the way she makes me feel sends a storm of emotions through my body that I'd felt so rarely before that they make me hungry for more.

The tip of her tongue drags across the smooth bottom of my cock all the way to where the crown meets the shaft, and while her hands toy with my balls and the trunk, she sends white-hot bliss through my spear by massaging the head with generous strokes. Her eyes open and look up at me through heavy lids, and I'm overwhelmed with a kind of attraction that shakes me to the core.

I tighten my grip on her hair, and I rock back and forth carefully, surprised she doesn't choke on how much of my cock she can handle. I'm a large man all over, and it takes skill to handle me. Juliette seems to know exactly how to get me going in ways even I never thought possible.

Or maybe she's just the right kind of curious.

I feel my balls tighten, and as she lets out a soft whimper, I feel the tension in my body well up and spring loose like a coil. The first shot of heavy, thick seed earns a moan from her as I feel my whole body wracked by the orgasm, and it shakes every muscle in my body as shot after shot follows it. She holds on tight and takes in as much as she can before pulling off for air, and more of my seed spills down her front. She grabs my cock without thinking about it and brings it to her lips again as I come, feeling each thick, potent throb spill more the hot, white seed onto her.

When it's over, I pull her up into my arms and press a kiss to her, feeling myself all over her front as her stiff nipples brush against the palms that grope them.

"Something for the road," she tells me with a satisfied smile up at me. "Since you helped me sleep the other night."

"Tit for tat," I tease, chuckling softly.

~

The smells of rich wood furnishings, frothing beers, and fried food fills our noses as we step into the English-style pub on the edge of Cheyenne where we agreed to hold our meeting. Breaker is at my side as both of us stride confidently into the restaurant, through the charming and inviting wood interiors and the crackling fire in the back.

"Nice ambience," Breaker says, and I chuckle.

Juliette is outside with Bones, who isn't officially part of this meeting. They're here in case Diesel demands proof that Juliette is alive, and if we're going to make a convincing case that she's here willingly, she needs to be here in person.

I damn sure hope she hasn't had a sudden change of heart between then and now, because she could ruin this whole meeting if she wants to. But she has to know this is for the best. I have faith in her that she'll make the right choice, if it crosses her mind.

It doesn't take us long to see a pair of familiar faces across the pub, but we don't slow down as we stare each other down on our way to where they're sitting.

Diesel and his officer Chainlink look almost too much like the way we last saw them, in the heat of battle outside the mine. I remember Ironside giving Diesel a parting gift to the chest before he escaped that battle with his tail between his legs. It *is* tempting to bring that up, but regardless, I'm surprised how well he's hiding his injury. He either heals fast, or he's forcing himself to put on a tough face.

The president of an MC like the Buzzsaws is always in a precarious position. He goes out of his way to draw the meanest motherfuckers from here to the Rockies, and keeping those kinds of guys in control is a challenge. I notice he's wearing a thick shirt that covers all the skin on his torso under his kutte. To be fair, it's cold out, but I can't help but wonder how Diesel is holding up under the surface.

For now, that surface is putting on a mean fucking face. He's glaring daggers at me from the moment we make eye contact, and there are no smiles on their faces as we take our seats across from them. There are already a couple of pints in front of them, and the server showed up before we so much as spoke to each other.

"Two stouts," Breaker says to the server, holding up two fingers. "Don't care what kind. Thanks."

The server seems to get the message that we're a *private* table, and after he brings our drinks, we're left alone.

"You looked better down the sights of a pistol," Breaker says, leaning back in his chair and smirking.

"You looked better fumbling to get a shot at me," Diesel grunts back, cracking a cruel smile at the corner of his mouth. "And I'd love to return the favor, so let's cut the bullshit. Why are you fucking around with my kin, Breaker?" He leans forward with a knit brow and adds, "Kidnapping ain't that noble of you, brother. Thought the high horse was what the Heartbreakers are all about."

"Maybe this is a business meeting after all, they've finally come around and got a proposal for us," Chainlink says, grinning.

"Oh, I got a *proposal*, alright," Breaker says, chuckling.

"Juliette is with me," I say, getting the others' attention immediately, and I meet both their gazes, especially Diesel's.

"Yeah, you seem like the right kind of ugly son of a bitch to do the job," Diesel says scornfully. "Don't they keep you on a leash these days?"

"Big Daddy's free to do whatever he wants," Breaker says coolly, not willing to give Diesel all the ground to flex nuts as much as he likes.

Meetings between MC leaders are serious business. To get guys like these to agree to an honorable meeting is a feat in and of itself. There's going to be some tension for dominance. The thought of Juliette is the only thing keeping either side from tearing the other apart.

"What I want to do is explain," I say in a firm, forceful tone that dominates the table instantly. I speak little in meetings for a reason. When I do, people listen. "She's with me willingly. She met up with me when she came back to take care of *your* mother."

"How did you-" Diesel starts to demand, his face turning red with anger.

"She told me," I say. "Because we've talked. A lot. If fact, I'd say she enjoys it--enough that she says yes when I asked her to marry me."

Chainlink spits his drink out to the side, and Diesel blinks his beady eyes at me, totally stupefied.

"We're engaged," I repeat slowly. "And she's with me because we're planning a wedding. Soon."

"I didn't come to this meeting to rub this shit in your face, as much as I'd like that, bud," Breaker says to Diesel after a long swig of his drink. "I'm not going to bullshit you and pretend like we get along, but this is what it is. I respect bonds, Diesel. Juliette thinks you do to. I want to propose a truce over the wedding."

"You're invited," I say, nodding. "Juliette wants this. If you want to see her to prove it, we're ready to do that."

Diesel stares at both of us in disbelief for a solid ten seconds, then looks to Chainlink briefly. They blink, Diesel raising his eyebrows, and he picks up his drink to knock back the rest of it before setting it down.

"Well, fuck me," he says in a low tone. "Guess that leaves me no choice...but to tell you two to go sit on an ice pick together, get comfortable, and suck my dick while you're at it," he says with a bright smile on his face, folding his hands in front of him before his face turns bright red. "You fuckin' serious? Why the hell would you think I care? I hate that bitch."

Our jaws drop, and it takes every ounce of strength in me not to lunge across the table at Diesel and slam his head into that glass.

"The hell?" Breaker blurts.

"Take that back before I cut your tongue out, fuckhead," I snarl at Diesel as I stand to my feet and plant both hands on the table between us.

In an instant, all three others at the table are up, and the rest of the pub looks our way with alarm as the tension in the room goes from neutral to fifth gear in the blink of an eye.

"Someone's got a crush," Diesel grunts, unimpressed. "Look man, I don't know what you see in her, but I don't give a shit what my sister does. I just want to know why you think you can fuck with my people and get away with it, but now I see you're too chickenshit to do that, either. Figured you'd at least shoot up mom's place and scare her out of bed," he says, chuckling like a teenager.

"You don't deserve a sister like her," I say in a bloodthirsty voice, thinking hard about going for the knife I hid in my boot before Diesel goes for the one he's probably got hidden in his.

"I think you deserve her just fine," he says with vague disgust, looking me up and down and snorting a laugh. "And don't you two think for a second I'll hesitate from making her a widow, either. If the bitch is stupid enough to let herself get swept up with dead men like you, she deserves whatever she gets."

"I'm going to melt down that fucking ring in your nose for our wedding bands," I growl, seeing red.

Just before I can reach across the table and make good on my promise, the doors of the pub fly open, and light floods in.

"Are you *fucking* serious?!" Juliette blurts, fire in her eyes as she crosses the restaurant to our table.

"You two couldn't keep things civil for five damn minutes, could you?" I blurt out angrily as I stumble into the pub. "Come on!" I groan.

Bikers, I swear to god. Why are they so intrinsically drawn to drama? It's like they're hardwired to pick fights with one another. I come storming through the door with my long black hair whipping out behind me. I'm amazed I was able to slip out of my guard's grasp, but then, I've always been pretty good at wiggling my way out of situations I don't want to be in. I march straight up to the table where Diesel and Daddy are seated, clearly on the verge of descent into punch-drunk chaos. I'm happy to have reached them before the first hook is thrown. Maybe I can intervene and stop this crazy train from rolling. But my elation is short-lived when I realize that Bones is barely a hair's breadth behind me, and I instantly feel his strong hands grab my arms from behind, yanking me back a little. I struggle in his grasp, kicking and grunting.

"Why are you holding *me* back? Stop them!" I cry out.

"Don't you dare let her go," Daddy growls.

I feel an arrow strike through my heart when he says those words. I feel betrayed. Wounded. Totally dazed. Bones tightens his grip on me and I feel that searing hot anger flare up inside of me.

"I thought you were going to give me some damn freedom," I snap.

He hisses back, "Not if you're just going to go dancing right back into danger."

"You poor idiot. Biting off way more than you can chew with that one there. She's always been a difficult girl to control," Diesel sneers.

"Control? You've never had control of me," I toss back. "I do what I want, not what you tell me to."

"Sure. You're an independent woman with her life all figured out. That's how you ended up right here: by making good choices," Diesel taunts me.

"I made good choices," I say through gritted teeth. "The best one was getting the hell away from that town. Away from all the bad memories. Away from you."

"Oh, step off," he scoffs. "I can't believe I ever let you follow your stupid little heart to Colorado.

What did you think was going to happen there? That you would just pull up your roots and plant yourself in that nice dark soil, turn into some beautiful fucking flower or whatever?"

Tears burn hotly in my eyes. I blink them away. I refuse to let that jerk see me cry. I won't give him the satisfaction.

"I wanted a chance at a normal life, okay? Is that so much to ask for?" I mumble.

"With our family? Our cursed lineage? Not a chance in hell," he replies, folding his arms over his chest.

"I should've known sharing a bloodline with you would mark me for bad luck," I toss right back. If he can come at me with swords I can at least hold up a knife. He shook his head in disgust.

"I thought maybe you weren't so bad when you finally gave up your stupid pipe dream of making it in Denver and came home to serve your family like you should've been doing all along," he growls.

"*Serve?* Excuse me?" I gasp indignantly.

"Yeah. I thought, 'oh good, she's come back to reality.' You were taking care of our useless mother. Cooking dinner. Keeping the house clean. Paying the bills and all that boring domestic shit. I liked that: knowing both my women kin were in the house where they belong," he jabs.

"Women kin? Useless? That's our mom you're

talking about. Since when do you talk like that?" I ask softly.

"A lot of things can change in seven years, Jules," he quips.

I feel the icy coldness of his stare deep down in my very soul and slithering frigidly through my veins.

"Who the hell are you anymore?" I whisper.

"Maybe if you had stuck around, you would know," Diesel snaps.

"I came back when I was needed! I'm the one at home taking care of Mom all day every day. I'm the one holding the threads of this messed up family together, just like always," I defend myself. "What more do you want from me?"

"Oh, don't pretend you ever gave a damn about me or your parents," he hisses.

"I came back," I repeat passionately. "To help!"

"Pfft. Yeah. Okay, sis. More like you've come back to spread your legs every time you hear a motorcycle ride by the house. Tell me, how long did you wait before jumping into bed with this goon?" he insults me.

Big Daddy immediately stands up to his full impressive height, knocking over a bar stool in the process. With his hands balling up into fists, he looms over a cool and calculated Diesel.

"Shut your mouth. Don't you talk about her that way," Daddy warns.

"She's my sister, I'll speak to her however I want," Diesel hurls back icily.

"Guys, cool it! We came here to do business, not to start a brawl!" I insist, trying to wrench away from Bones so I can step between the two men who had been the most important in my world in recent times.

Diesel flat out laughs, looking at me with a mixture of pity and resentment. It scares me down to the core to see that look on his face. My heart sinks as it dawns on me that there are no traces left of the young man I used to recognize as my rebellious but still totally human older brother. Now he seems almost beastlike, his eyes completely devoid of any emotion or warmth. Everything from his smirking lips to his sniveling nose and furrow brow speaks of bitterness. I can't help but feel a twinge of guilt. What if it is my fault that he's like this? What if the strain and hurt of my abandonment was the catalyst that hardened his heart and turned him into the evil, twisted up cyclone of a man he is today?

The thought is nearly enough to make me crumble. The idea that my desperate bid for freedom in Colorado could've ruined everything is a painful one to swallow. I feel like I could drown in the depths of my regret and shame. But I'm zapped back to reality by the menacing way Diesel stands up and puffs out his chest, preening and trying to intimidate Big

Daddy. Panic swirls up in my gut as I watch them glare each other down.

"And then you had to come back and cause more trouble by cavorting around the place with the enemy," Diesel snarls. "Making me look like a chump."

"You've got it backwards," Daddy breaks in.

"Excuse me?" is the cold response.

"You heard me. You cannot blame Juliette for your own shitty decision making. The only reason she's ended up in my arms is because you've forced her there," Daddy insists.

I wonder if he truly believes that. It makes my heart ache. I wish I could assure him that what I feel for him is greater than our circumstances, stronger than the forces that brought me into his protection. But not right now. I have an all-out fight to defuse.

"If you won't keep her safe, I will," Big Daddy says sharply. "You can count on that."

"I couldn't care less about her safety. You can have her. Do whatever you want with her. She's already ruined, you know. I bet she sucked every cock she met in Colorado," Diesel cackles.

I feel my face burn hot with humiliation. I open my mouth to deny it all, but it's like I'm frozen in place. Too stunned to do a thing to stop the dominoes from falling.

"You slimy bastard. I'll warn you one more time

not to talk about Juliette that way. Hell, don't talk about any woman that way," Big Daddy growls.

"Oh, because you're a shining example of chivalry yourself? Yeah. Right," Diesel retorts.

"Simmer down," hisses Bones from behind me.

"Don't tell me what to do," my brother barks.

"You know, none of this would've happened if you had just stayed on the straight and narrow like I did!" I blurt out suddenly, unable to hold it back.

"You're a good girl now, huh? Is that what you're selling these days? You're not fooling anybody," he snipes.

"You got all tangled up with that goddamn bike club. Fell in with the wrong crowd," I accuse.

"Sis, I *am* the wrong crowd. I am the one you all should fear," he declares.

"You have no idea what you're even saying," Daddy scoffs. "All you are is a failure of a brother and a disgrace of a son."

"Oh no," I breathe, watching the colors change from shocked pale to apoplectic red on Diesel's face.

"How dare you talk about my family?" he growls.

"It's true!" I burst out.

"You're siding with him again?" Diesel snarls angrily.

In the next several seconds, a lot of things happen at once. Diesel lunges at Big Daddy, preparing to swing at his face. But Bones releases me and jumps to restrain Diesel as Daddy ducks masterfully out of the way. Diesel shrugs out of Bones's grip and manages to spit bitterly at the ground before storming out of the pub in a huff. To my relief, nobody goes after him. Not until the guy called Chainlink stalks out of the pub a few moments later, looking determined and resigned.

I feel totally dazed and wracked with guilt and rage in almost equal measure. I could tell that it's the fact that his own sister, someone he views as inherently beneath him, has called him out in front of everyone, that has him the most ruffled. I get the sense everybody else is aware of it, too. I'm still stunned with anger and hurt when finally Bones judges the coast is clear and Big Daddy leads me out of the pub. We take off on his motorcycle, rumbling off down the quiet highway while I stew in my bitter feelings.

By the time we get home, I'm still seething. In fact, I feel like my negative emotions have just been building up the whole ride back.

"You're shaking like a leaf. You feel okay?" Daddy asks as he helps me dismount the bike.

"I'm just pissed off, that's all," I admit.

"You need to calm down. You're going to work yourself up and get sick," he warns me gently.

"I can't calm down! I feel like I'm about to explode!" I confess, feeling that annoying lump in my throat again.

"You need a release," he says.

"God, yes. Something. Anything," I whimper.

Without another word, Big Daddy lifts me up into his arms and carries me inside the house. He takes me straight to the kitchen and hoists me up onto the counter. Before I can even make sense of things, he's pulling down my underwear and hiking up my skirt. His thigh wedges mine apart and I sigh with anticipation.

"Do it. Fuck me hard and fast," I hiss.

"Gladly," he growls. "Hold on tight."

I do what I'm told. Big Daddy unbuttons his jeans and tugs them down enough to let his cock bounce free. He barely has to touch my cunny before I'm dripping wet and ready for him. He teases my sensitive clit while he slowly slides the full length of his enormous shaft inside of me. I groan and press into him, silently begging for more. Always more. I can never get enough.

Daddy pounds into me mercilessly, keeping me on the edge of the counter to hit my g-spot over and over again. Every time, I feel the anger in my body decrease and the excitement increase. Everything is just better with him. Everything feels so damn good.

He kisses me deeply as he spears my tight little pussy, both of us rocking and moaning in tandem, working ever upward to the heights of intense pleasure. It doesn't take long for me to reach the edge, and as I grasp at his shoulders for balance, I feel his muscular body tense up and his cock pumps my fertile flower full of his sticky seed. I gush all over his cock, my juices running and mixing with his as they slide down my thighs and drip onto the kitchen floor.

As we get cleaned up, we trot off to the bathroom together and this time he runs a luxurious bath. We sink into the tub together, with my back resting against his chest. He softly kisses the top of my head.

"So," he murmurs, "are you still down for our little fake wedding?"

I nod eagerly. "Yes. I'm sure now. Diesel may act cold, but I know it's got to reach him deep down. If we could have any chance at all of saving lives, it's worth it. Right?" I suggest.

At least, that's my excuse for now. Surely my desire to stick with Big Daddy has nothing to do with how amazing the sex is. Not at all.

BIG DADDY

The orange sun burns low in the sky on my wedding day, and I still can't believe I'm able to think that thought so soon in my life.

Marriage isn't something I've put on the table for me. Even though the wedding is fake, the tuxedo I'm wearing under my kutte is definitely not, and neither are the roaring engines of my groomsmen all around me.

I'm leading the pack with Breaker, my best man, and every other member of the Heartbreakers MC is thundering across the highway with me, all of them dressed to impress by biker standards. This day came as fast as we could make preparations for it, but the turnout is more impressive than I ever could have expected.

We're not just showing up to town, we're making an entrance they'll remember for a long time.

Mayor Hartley was on board with the idea from the second Breaker proposed a public marriage. After some negotiations about organizing and a donation to the mayor's election fund, we came out of the meeting with what might as well have been a parade under our authority. It turns out that the mayor is about as desperate for an opportunity to feel some life in the town, since things have been nothing but either boring or dangerous for as long as a lot of people can remember.

The town is small, but the main street is fenced off, and a number of curious townsfolk have gathered to see the entourage rolling into town, all our engines firing off like a steady storm blowing in. They look on with mixed faces, some in awe, some excitement, some fear as we carve a path down the main street. My groomsmen and I--five in total, since Tank earned his place helping out with my bride--ride ahead of the rest of the pack in formation, and we look dressed to kill.

All of us bear our kuttes proudly, and I have a banner mounted on the back of my ride that displays the colors proudly. I'm not the only one in a tux, either. That was one of Juliette's requirements for going along with this stunt. That and one other thing.

The town isn't a place anyone would call fancy, but I've come to love it, and the modest but charming community garden in the center of town is the fanciest venue there is next to the clubhouse itself. It was tempting to hold it there, but we want this to be a community thing, not just a club one.

If we want the town on our side in this war, we need to be a part of them.

Our bikes reach town square as the orange grows a deeper hue, casting a glow over our gleaming black motorcycles as we come to a halt in formation two by two. A formation of motorcycles soon takes up most of the space around the square, except for an entryway to the town hall across the street.

There are decorations around the garden, mostly ribbons and bouquets of flowers from the local shops, all arranged tidily around the place to make it look like it was made for hosting something like this. It's autumn, and by god, it feels like it. The golden and orange trees lining the square sway gently in the breeze, leaves adorn the ground everywhere, and pumpkins and other gourds are piled outside a lot of the businesses and homes we can see from here. A trellis arch in the middle of the garden near a small pond stands waiting, and I have to admit, my heart is thumping hard at the sight.

"Ready for this, big guy?" Breaker says as we dismount and start making our way into position.

"Oh yeah," I growl, smiling up at the sight. "Hell of a lot more than I expected. Feels pretty damn good."

"Careful talking like that," he says, chuckling. "She might actually fall for you."

The club members all take their seats quickly, and we get into our positions around the altar. As planned, Mayor Hartley himself meets me under the trellis, giving me a nod as he stands ready in a fine, tailored suit.

There's no person better suited to the occasion to marry us.

With my groomsmen lined up at my side, I feel like I'm standing on top of a mountain, looking out on all the faces of the rest of the MC I've grown to love and fight alongside. They're all men who've taken up arms for a good cause, and as long as we ride, we'll keep pushing that cause.

It's wild that as much as I love all the bastards, they're not even half the real reason my heart is racing.

When the music starts, I get a lump in my throat, and I watch the doors of city hall open. Juliette's one other condition was specifically because her mother doesn't know anything about this wedding (and wouldn't, since our names won't be published), so there's no chance she'll see her.

Kate, Lauren, and Justine, the three women Breaker, Bones, and Ironside has met up with and fallen hard for over the past few months, come out first as the bridesmaids for the wedding. I don't know how much they've gotten to know the bride, but I've been worrying constantly about her comfort while she's away from me, so I hope they get along at the least. They seem happy enough that they must, anyway.

They take their positions at the other side of the lineup, and I give them grateful smiles as they pass and my attention snaps to the doors as the music changes.

Juliette steps out in a raven-black wedding dress that hugs her figure beautifully, and I feel my rugged face split into an ear-to-ear smile as we make eye contact across the path to me. Music guides her as she walks in long, proud strides that I memorize every moment of in her eyes.

It's fake, I have to remind myself. This is just for the act. It's a PR stunt. It's to help her family, and to help her by extension. I can't let my mind wander to all the dark places it wants to in the even darker folds of that dress.

But damn, she must be a good actress.

Her eyes hold me locked to them almost the entire walk up the makeshift aisle. Her perfectly styled hair frames them beautifully, and her makeup is nothing short of flawless. There's desire in her eyes, and her cheeks are blushing. Her face almost looks surprised at herself. If she's taken aback by how good this evening feels, then that's one more thing we have in common.

She reaches me at last, and the way she smiles up

at me through her veil is trembling, trying to stay calm. I wink down at her, and she gives a laugh that is definitely just a cover-up for a half-sob. Her shaky smile grows broader, and after she sniffs and takes a breath, she gets a hold of herself, and we laugh softly. It ripples through the audience, infectious.

"Thank you all for gathering here on yet another one of our beautiful sunsets," the mayor says with a broad smile. "It does my heart good to see the community get together under such a wonderful occasion, and at a time of year known for the start of winter, let's embrace the spirit of new life and new beginnings."

Considering more than one of the bridesmaids is expecting, it's a fitting message. The crowd, now mixed with townspeople joining in, applauds briefly.

"We're gathered here to join Juliette Rideau and Jason...ahem, 'Big Daddy' Porter in matrimony," he says, legally obligated to use my real name, to my chagrin. "The two have written their own vows, and will exchange them now."

I clear my throat, and Juliette looks on, genuinely curious about what a couple of people who've known each other for so little time can say to each other for something that should be as meaningful as this. Acting or no, this feels meaningful.

I feel every nerve in my body not calm exactly, but I feel focused, settled, and more ready than ever before.

"Juliette," I say in my deep but clear voice that carries surprisingly well. "We met a lifetime ago. At least, it feels that way. Now it feels like the start of a new one. I'm glad I kept you in my heart all that time we were apart. I love you, baby girl."

Juliette's face is steady, but her eyes are wide and sincere. I might have let a little too much of the heart slip into that fake wedding vow. For a few moments, she's lost for words, but she recovers with a deep breath as she swallows and speaks.

"Jason," she says, making the goosebumps on the back of my neck prick up. "I've had you on my mind a lot more than either of us knew. You took me into the shadows, and you made me want to stay there. I love you, Daddy."

My heart melts. I don't know whether to be overjoyed that I get to have this moment with my Juliette, or bitter at the irony of the universe that's bringing this beautiful day to my life as part of one big sham. I don't know if I care right at this second. I'm going to live in the moment, and the moment has me lifting the veil off Juliette's face and bringing those smiling lips to mine.

There's a warm rush that swells in me as we kiss, and butterflies swell up in my stomach. Neither of us can stop grinning at each other as the audience cheers around us, and I lead Juliette down to my own motorcycle, which has been decked out hurriedly in black decor and flowers with the subtle JUST MARRIED tags on the back of it.

I kiss Juliette one more time before getting us both on, and with a fierce rev of my engine, I lead the pack that files out behind me all the way to the clubhouse.

"Okay, that was actually pretty nice," she says as we ride, still laughing delightedly. "Pretty *really* nice. Thanks for the best fake wedding ever, honey."

"Best fake bride ever," I growl back at her with a chuckle. "And you keep that dress on, baby girl. I want to take it off of you tonight."

I feel her shiver at that, and it makes me all the more excited for when we get to the clubhouse.

As soon as we've all pulled up, all bets are off. The bikers flood the place with any of the more adventurous townsfolk who want to see if they can party with bikers for one hell of a reception.

"Oh my god," she says as we step downstairs, eyes widening at the lavish decor that Kate worked hard on all around the bar. It looks more like a real-ass reception venue than a biker bar. "She really went all out!"

"The wedding might be fake, but the party sure isn't," I say with a wink.

As people bustle in and we get our first drinks of the night, the spirits can't be higher. I see Breaker coming in with a smiling and chattering Mayor Hartley, telling me that our worries about the town are going to be well taken care of by the time the night's over.

Drinks are on us tonight, so as the booze starts flowing, the spirits get higher--and the spirits do plenty of flowing, too. Juliette and I share our first bite of wedding cake together, and instead of smashing it in her face, I swipe a little on her neck and lean in to kiss it off--to her delight and the wolf whistles of the crowd.

Music plays, friends get made, and people get drunk. It's more than I ever could have wanted at my own wedding. And my bride is more woman than I'd ever dream for. We barely get a chance to talk the whole time, unsurprisingly. Tonight is about the people.

Except for one.

"My man!" Bones says, staggering toward me as I hold Juliette away, chuckling. "I got somethin' here for you," he slurs, taking an envelope out of his kutte and grinning, waggling his eyebrows. "I know this wedding is, y'know, but fuck man, I don't want you to think I don't appreciate you."

"Ah, shut up, Bones," I chuckle.

"No I mean it!" he blurts, sticking the envelope toward me. "Take it! Weddin' present."

I open it, and I'm genuinely stunned by what I see.

"This is money," I say.

"The money I owe you for pool," he says, smiling more sincerely at me.

I stare at him for a moment, then embrace him tight, feeling him sniff, and I pat him on the back.

"Brother," I say, nodding to him.

"Brother," he says back, dabbing his eyes as he heads back to the crowd as I beam.

"What was that?" Juliette asks.

"Long story," I say as the music changes, and I nod to the dance floor. "Sounds like we have a first dance to take care of.

She grins, and I lead her out to the center of the floor, where we sway softly together in the warm lights of the bar, and it's hard to tear each other's eyes off one another.

The whole night is such a storm that feels so deeply, acutely real that I don't know which way is up by the time I decide I've had my fill of it. But that moment comes exactly after I take the garter off, and as soon as we have a moment to escape, I whisper into Juliette's ear as I tug her toward the private rooms.

"Let's get a little privacy."

JULIETTE

My heart is pounding like crazy as I feel my new husband's hand smooth down the slope of my waist. I shiver and shake under his touch, the adrenaline already beginning to pump through my veins. He knows just how to move me, how to teach my body lessons and show me the light with the simplest brush of a hand. It feels so right, having him near me. Having him whisper to me and caress my soft skin like I'm his secret lover. Only there's no secret now. Not from the townspeople and our new shared "found" family of the Heartbreakers and their assorted friends, loves, and allies, at least. There's still my mother who is being intentionally kept out of the loop, but other than that, it's all out in the open now. We have a literal crowd of witnesses to back us up. There is a small but significant amount of photographic evidence to prove what happened. Proof of what we just pledged to one another. I may have been wearing a black dress and the circumstances are anything but normal, but it was a wedding nonetheless.

I can still hardly wrap my mind around the fact that I just promised my heart and soul to this man I barely know. I've always been so independent. Not to mention extremely protective of that independence. It's why I ran away to Denver to begin with. So I could finally live for myself and do as I pleased. Follow my heart, as my brother so coldly explained it. And I can't pretend like he's wrong about that. I did follow my heart. Or rather, the deep pangs of desire for freedom and separation from my difficult memories that I felt in my heart when I made that decision. I still feel flutters of that desire now. It's like a feral creature returning hopelessly to the wild. The road calls me. Adventure calls me. But so does stability and comfort. I just want to travel the world and find out where is best to build a nest.

Of course, it will have to be different now that I've given myself up to a handsome, powerful man. It's no longer only about what I want, what I need. It's about both of us and striking a balance. It's about compromise. That's what I've always heard, anyway. I may not have all the usual jaded relatives and hopeless romantic friends to tell me that I'm entering a fairytale or leaving one. Like in all those wedding movies. Rom coms packed with eclectic family members and outrageous wedding guests. Humor and depth. The emotional roller coaster. But our relationship hasn't been like that. We haven't had time to embark on a magical, epic-length love story. Ours is shortened. Abbreviated to a sharp, gleaming point. It's a barbed wire fence rather than a trellis of creeping flowers to arch over our ceremony and bathe us in wholesome light. There are wholesome moments to our dynamic, to be sure. Daddy is a shockingly affectionate person. There is more softness between us than most people might expect just by looking at us.

And since I'm just now getting to know him, there's no telling whether we will click into place and suddenly want the same things or just fall apart. We barely had time to get to know each other. What can we possibly expect?

Except that it doesn't feel that way. Big Daddy doesn't feel like a stranger to me. Our relationship— our marriage, I remind myself with a jolt— doesn't feel fake or forced. Maybe our wedding is just a tactical move on the club's part. Maybe it is all just for show and I'm being a hopeless romantic by reading too much into it all. But I can't help it. I feel how I feel, whether it's advisable or not. Whether I'll end up getting burned or not I'm in it to win it, and I'm overjoyed to find myself on the same team as Daddy. I know that no matter how severe things get,

I can be certain that everything will end up working out as long as he's with me.

It's strange, actually, coming to the slow realization that I don't have to be one-hundred-percent in control at all times. I've gotten so used to being the fixer for other people, I forget to step back and just let things happen sometimes. It's hard for me to relinquish control. I just want to do things right, and for much of my life, that has meant doing it myself. Building my own means of making money. Finding myself a whole brand new city to start over in. Being my own champion, my own cheerleader. And then, of course, there's all the hours of determination and perseverance I've put in on behalf of my family. Keeping the peace. Defusing the fights. Cleaning the house. Paying bills, washing clothes, cooking every meal. Trying to keep my mom happy and healthy. Trying not to let my brother come blowing into our neat little lives like the tornado he has always been and destroy what little stability I molded for us to live on. It's not that I feel used or anything. In fact, I view taking care of my mom as just an expectation of being her daughter. Our lives haven't always been easy, especially after my father passed, but she's done her best for me, and it's only right for me to return that favor.

But now that I have met Big Daddy, I'm learning how good it can feel to just give it up for a while. Let someone else take the reins. And for the first time in my life, I find myself in the care of someone actually truly capable to do the job right. It takes a little convincing, but he's definitely proven himself a worthy caretaker. It's just hard to unlearn the instinct to take charge. For so long I've lived on the very precarious fine line between "doing okay" and "falling to pieces." It's an exhausting line to walk. The weight of everything presses down on me so hard, but it's a burden I'm used to. You never know how heavy a weight you're carrying until someone lifts it off your shoulders.

Daddy is that person for me. Even though I fought him hard for it at the start, I'm beginning to see now the benefits of letting him help me. Even this wedding, however false or sudden it might be, somehow went off without a hitch. And in such a tight turnaround, too! I still don't understand how he managed to pull it off. Most men wouldn't have a clue how to stage a wedding, even when it's a real marriage and not a spontaneous truce decision. But then, Big Daddy isn't like most men. He's thoughtful but decisive. Powerful but gentle. Totally wild, of course, like all apex predators. But he can still bring himself down to the nitty gritty of a faux-domestic life to complete the picture. He's more calculating than he looks, and I find it incredibly comforting. I know he can take care of me. And even more amazingly, I know he wants to take care of me. I can feel it in every buzzing, thrumming touch of his hands on my body. In the way he looks at me with such fire and passion. Hell, even just the way he says the three syllables of my name. He lingers over them like they taste like honey on his tongue. I always thought my name was kind of clunky. Unusual. But when Daddy says it, I hear the ringing bell of beauty. It's like a song. And there is no more beautiful music to me than the low growl of his voice against my ear.

I'm a lucky girl. That's for sure. Real or fake, I could not have designed a better husband for myself in a lab. He may not be perfect, but he's perfect for me. It's odd to realize how long we have technically been aware of each other. I was so young when I first set eyes on him. I smile to think about it, how I had no idea what the future was going to bring. How important— even vital— this man would become for me in less than a decade. It's like he's been there all along, a seed quietly and casually planted but with a delayed bloom. Now, though, that plant has sprouted and is growing like a weed, resplendent foliage reaching high and proud into the wide blue sky of Wyoming. Flowers blossoming against the bright sun. Leaves trembling in the dew. We are strong and getting stronger every day. I draw so much strength from Daddy without even realizing it. It's like having a second backbone even tougher than my own, a safety net I know for a fact will cushion me if I fall. He's always looking out for me, and if I have to rush into this marriage to keep him watching over me, then so be it. I can't deny that it's addicting, intoxicating in a way.

I feel so strong. I feel safe. Even with the sad realization that my own brother ignored my request for him to attend my wedding. Oh, and the fact that Diesel is maniacally evil. I used to think he was just regular mean, the kind of elbow-in-the-ribs obnoxious everyone's big brother seems to be. But over time, it's become more and more obvious that he isn't a harmless jerk. He's a *dangerous* jerk. And I shudder to think that I just let him into our home, in the same room as our delicate, overly forgiving mother.

"You look pale," Daddy says suddenly, bringing me back to the current moment as we step through the doorway of the suite we're staying in. He lays a gentle hand on my shoulder and I lean into him instinctively.

"Sorry. Got a little lost in my thoughts for a minute there," I assure him, forcing a smile.

But he's not dissuaded. As usual, he can see right through my facade. He gives me a serious, contemplative look as he closes the door.

"Thoughts about what? Clearly something is upsetting you, Juliette. You can tell me things. We *are* married now," he reminds me, not without a hint of amusement.

"Good point. But that doesn't mean you have to

listen to me whine about my fears and worries," I say.

"Do I have to? No. But I want to. Let me help you, sweetheart. You know I can," he reminds me.

I smile, more genuinely this time.

"I know. You've shown me that again and again," I relent. "I guess I'm just a little, shall we say, bummed."

"Bummed? The ceremony went off without issue. We were convincing," he says.

"Not about that. The wedding was fantastic. You're fantastic. The way the Heartbreakers have embraced me is fantastic. All of this is...so much more than I deserve," I gush.

"You deserve only the best. Always," Daddy says firmly. He brushes a loose tendril of hair back out of my face, peering into my eyes with pure affection. I know it's futile to try and hide my feelings from him.

"Diesel didn't even show up," I admit. "I really held out hope that he might listen to reason and come to the wedding. At least roll up in time for the toasts."

"Well, he's never been especially attentive to the wants and needs of others, even the ones closest to him," he answers astutely.

"I know. You're right. It's just hard to accept that someone I grew up with, who's known me since I was born, could brush me off so easily," I sigh. "I thought maybe he would put aside this warring faction crap and just come see his sister in white."

"Well, you did wear black," he remarks.

"True. Maybe if I wore white he would've shown up," I joke half-heartedly. I can't even joke about it quite yet. It's still a little raw.

"It's his loss," he assures me. "And remember that you are not responsible for the shitty choices your brother makes. You're not his keeper. You don't have to worry about anybody but yourself."

"What about my mom?" I venture quietly. I haven't realized until this moment how nervous I've been about that. But as usual, Daddy knows just how to coax me out of my shell. I don't know how he does it.

"She's being looked after. She's doing fine," he reassures me. "I promise."

And somehow, despite the nagging little voices of doubt in the back of my mind, I believe him.

"Thank you. And I'm sorry I'm so full of worry," I mumble.

"You're used to taking care of everybody else," he says accurately. "But you don't have to worry about that anymore. I'm here now. You'll never have to worry again. I've got you. And I won't let you fall."

He pulls me into a tight embrace. I tilt my head back to smile up at him. /My eyes lock with his and immediately I can feel all the anxiety easing out of my body. I feel lighter and brighter just having his arms around me.

"Wow. I'm your wife," I murmur, totally awed.

He grins and strokes my hair gently, leaning in to kiss me.

"Yes, you are," he growls. "And I will protect you no matter what. You're mine now."

"I was always yours. Ceremony or not," I mumble against his lips.

He kisses me deeply, his hands smoothing down the slope of my hips and around to grab my ass. I feel a sharp tingle of desire roll through me. He lights me up without even having to try. But when he lifts me up and carries me in my black bridal gown to the bed, it's more than innocent affection coursing through my veins. I want him with a fierceness I've never known before, and he gives me back the same exact energy.

"I know exactly what you need," he purrs.

I brace myself up on my elbows as I watch him push up the skirt and netting of my bridal gown. I bite my lip, already tensing with anticipation of what's to come.

BIG DADDY

I've never known peace like this.

It's like I can feel myself sleeping, but time doesn't mean anything as long as I feel that warmth by my side. That's the brand of abstract bullshit that goes through my head over the night after the best sex I'd had in my life.

Maybe I held command in bed last night, but Juliette still knocked me back onto my ass harder than I'd ever fallen before. And goddamn, I'm glad she did.

It was impossible not to think about the fact that we're legally husband and wife. That was my wife I was feeling wrapped around my thick cock last night. Just the memory of it in that weird state between dreaming and sleeping got me hard again. Every second of the day is burned into my mind, and I can't help but play it over in my head in my sleep. I can't control my dreams, and they're focused on one thing alone.

She'd be a perfect wife. That's not even my wishful thinking, that's a statement of fact. She doesn't take anyone's shit, she's smart as hell, she's funny, and she can handle herself when the going gets hard.

The hard truth is I don't think there's any man in the world who could keep up with her. As for me, well, I only just married her. But lying here in bed next to her after a consummation like that has made me wonder what's on her mind for the future. I can't imagine she'll play along long after this war is over. Time will tell.

Just as those warm thoughts are turning to doubt, the sounds of the usual morning stirring upstairs wakes me up at last. I flex my hands under my pillow, smiling warmly as I feel my nude body in the warm sheets, and I reach over to scoop Juliette into my arms.

My hand brushes over an empty, cool patch of sheets.

Eyes springing open, I sit up in bed and look around. I'm alone. Juliette is nowhere to be seen. Confused, I look to the door and see it shut. Her bridal gown is still here, but her daytime clothes are missing along with her purse.

My face pales. No, you've got to me shitting me, right?

I get dressed in a hurry and head into the hall, pulling my kutte over my shoulders as I pass Kate at the bar on her cell phone.

"Hey, how's the new husband?" she asks cheerfully as I walk by.

"Looking for the new wife," I grunt. "Have you seen Juliette anywhere?"

When she shakes her head, I get a bad feeling, and I head upstairs with my heart pounding. I search up and down the clubhouse, the conference room, both the bars, and even everywhere upstairs in a near frenzy.

I'm almost six and a half feet tall, when I get to stomping around the place like I'm on a mission, people make way for me. And I'm thorough. She's not here.

I step outside, running a hand over my head with a clenched jaw as the cold morning air greets me and wakes me up. At the end of the parking lot row, I see Skid, one of the members, about to light up a cigarette while sitting on his bike. He's a scrawny little guy, but he has a good head on his shoulders.

"Hey," I grunt.

"Hey man, congrats!" he says, giving me a wave as I approach. "I prolly got a cigar around here somewhere left over from last night if you want."

"I'm good," I grunt. "You were on guard early this morning, weren't you? Did you see my wife anywhere?"

"Oh yeah," he says, and my heart pounds twice as hard. "She was out here just before dawn when she slipped out. She'd called a cab, said she was going to grab her car. She left it parked by the uh, city hall or whatever, where the wedding was."

"Did she come back with it?" I ask, feeling a vein pulse in my forehead.

"N-no," Skid said, slowly realizing something is very wrong. "What's up, chief?"

My first instinct is to reach forward and rip Skid's head clean off his neck, but I hold myself back. I have to remember that the rest of the gang doesn't know she's a prisoner. Everyone but the officers and Tank thinks that wedding was totally real, and that I'm a happily married man to a loving wife. To him, there was nothing suspicious about what Juliette did.

"Nothing," I grunt in a tense voice thick with restraint. "Just...worried about her is all. I'm going after her, if you catch wind of her, you call me immediately. Not Breaker, me," I say, jabbing a thumb at myself with a fierce look as I stride over to my own motorcycle.

"You got it, chief!" Skid calls before I start the engine and roar off.

After a short ride through town, where I see the cleaners have already taken down all the mess from the wedding and the procession, I reach the town square and the garden. The arch is still up, and I come to a stop at a position where I can look through it to the town hall that Juliette came down, and it brings a smile to my lips and a break from my fears for just a moment.

Those fears come back hard. Her car is nowhere to be seen. I remember seeing it during the wedding yesterday in passing, and that whole lot is empty now. I drive by the impoundment lot just in case, but it hasn't been towed, either.

I come to a stop on my bike by the roadside and lean on the handles with one arm, rubbing my temples with the other.

"Fuck," I murmur. "Fuck!" I roar more loudly, unable to hold back the frustration.

She saw an opening, and she took it. I can't fucking believe it. It's impossible, I must be missing something. But the evidence seems pretty fucking damning, and I've got no one but myself to blame. She played me, and I should have seen it coming. If it had been anyone else, I'd have seen it coming.

But not from her. I don't feel betrayed, I feel angry at myself for not expecting it. The one time I let my guard down, it bites me in the ass.

I've always been a suspicious guy, but she found a way to relax me that I'd never known before. That can't be meaningless, there's got to be another expla-nation for what she did. I take out my phone and check it, but unsurprisingly, there are no messages from her, just the same wave of congratulations from the club members I saw when I checked this morning.

I call her, and it goes to voicemail over and over again. I send her a curt text asking where she went, and as I do, I hear the sound of another motorcycle rumbling behind me.

I turn to see Bones coming to a halt at my side, giving me finger-guns. "What's going on, brother? Heard you ran this way in a storm after your girl, everything alright?"

"Everything's not alright, Bones," I grunt. "She's gone."

Bones's jaw drops, and the mirth leaves his face. "Shit," he murmurs. "Like-"

"Gone gone," I say. "It was smart. I should have kept her prisoner. Should have had the wedding private. At the cabin."

"Hey," Bones says as he jabs a finger at me. "Stop beating yourself up before I start beating you up."

"I'd like to see you try," I growl.

"Alright, easy Goliath, I know you're tense," Bones says, taking the joke out of his tone. "We'll find her. But the real reason I'm here is Breaker wants a meeting, and that means we need to get back to the clubhouse. Four heads are better than one, and they'll want to know too."

That sounds as good as anything else to me right now, so the two of us roar off back to church.

Downstairs in the conference room ten minutes

later, the tone is no more grim than the rest of the morning has been. Breaker has the map of the state down on the table in front of us, where Ironside and Bones and I loom over it. The only welcome sight in the room is the mountain of breakfast biscuit sandwiches Ironsides brought along for the meeting.

"Here's where we stand," Breaker says in a firm, clear tone--an authoritative tone he only uses when he's prepping the troops for battle, I've come to learn over the years. I don't blame him. That time is upon us.

"Diesel has thrown our peace offer back in our faces without a second thought," Breaker starts. "He did not walk out of that meeting we had without knowing exactly what it meant. There's going to be blood. He's giving us no choice. Ironside, I had you scouting out strip clubs out on the western borders of our territory, update the others on what you've told me."

"We know at least three places Diesel and his riders use for their operations," the veteran tells us, pointing to three knives stabbed into the map (the table has seen its share of abuse over the years). "We also know that his latest base of operations isn't safe for him anymore thanks to us, so he's on the move again, but we know he uses these places in some form or another."

"They're drop-off points," Breaker says. "And we

have a tip that a new victim is being moved through the state as we speak."

"Are we sure about the tip?" I ask.

"Very," Breaker says, "I've got one of their civilian contacts on take."

"Wonder if this is the girl who went missing right out of Yellowstone," Bones says.

"I'd bet money on it," Breaker says. "You saw her on the news, she's exactly the type they'd go for. And if it's the same girl, she's been missing for little enough time that we might be able to catch her at any three of these points as they move her across the state. They know we're at war, but they don't know we're watching their supply lines."

"Hit 'em where they tried to hit us," I say with a menacing smile. "We can have eyes on the western-most outpost here, Point A, since that should be the first place she's headed. As soon as we get word that they're moving her to Point B, we have some riders raise some hell at Point C. The Buzzsaws will send riders to Point C, we retreat, and meanwhile someone will have hit Point B hard and fast and get the girl out of there."

The others pause for a moment, staring at me, and Breaker has a smile on his face.

"Alright, General," Bones finally says with a chuckle. "You're making the rest of us look bad!"

"I like that plan," Breaker says, crossing his arms.

"Solid advice, I think we should put some serious thought into it. Everyone else?"

"Aye," the other two say in unison.

"You seem different," Ironsides says, always straight to the point.

"Think that might have something to do with the elephant in the room," Bones says, giving me a nod, and the smile fades from my face as I look to Breaker.

"I have bad news," I say. "Juliette is gone."

Breaker's face darkens. "What do you know?"

"She slipped out at dawn, got her car, and I haven't had a chance to pick up the trail since," I say. "But she's been gone for hours, she could be anywhere."

"Any idea why?" Ironside asks.

I'm silent for a few moments. I know what my instinct is, but that's not me anymore. The guys are right, I feel different than usual. It's subtle, but it's strong, and with a clear head, I know what I need to do.

"No," I say. "But I don't think she has betrayed us."

That draws raised eyebrows all around the room.

"This looks pretty traitorous, I'm not gonna lie," Bones points out.

"It does," I say, looking him in the eye. "But even though that wedding was a sham, I know her better than anyone else in this room. We need to look for her, but she's *my* fucking wife, and we will *not* treat her like any less than that until I get proof otherwise from her own mouth."

Breaker looks more impressed than anything. "Granted," he says simply.

"I'll look for her personally," I go on. "This is a situation I started without club permission, and I accept the responsibility for handling it."

"What does this change mean for all this?" Ironside says, gesturing back down to the map.

"It could be nothing," Breaker says, frowning down at the map. "She might run off and go back to her old life after this."

"Or she could tell Diesel that whole wedding was fake," Ironside says. "That'll make us look weak, and he'll know to come after the town twice as hard."

"I'll find her before she can do that, if that's what she's planning," I say firmly.

"Alright," Breaker says. "That's enough for now, we'll regroup tonight after the search. Bones, Ironside, you two give us some privacy," he adds, and as the two nod and stalk out, I stare at Breaker across the table in silence.

"You care about her," Breaker says bluntly when the door is shut.

"Yeah," I say bluntly. "I do."

"You're serious about this?" he asks raising an eyebrow. "You think it's not just you? I need you to be sure. Damn sure. There are lives at stake in this war, and whether you like it or not, the two of you are tangled up in the middle of it. I need to know where you stand."

I slowly walk around the table to Breaker and look him in the eye.

"I care about her enough to stand by her as her husband and look out for her by any means necessary," I say. "Even if that means tracking her down and taking her again."

"You're my enforcer, brother," Breaker says, nodding to me. "I trust you. And I can tell this is more than just a one-time thing, I can see it in your eyes. I just needed to hear it from your mouth."

A sudden pounding at the door gets our attention, and before we can say another word, a pale young man sticks his head through the door--one of our scouts. "Shit, sorry to interrupt," he says. "But there have been shots fired on some of our riders out by Ucross!"

"Ucross?" Breaker growls. "Fuck, that's one of these points!" he says, gesturing down to the map with the drop-off points marked, and he looks over at me with a curt nod. "Gather the men. We're riding. Now."

I nod, and I head past the scout upstairs, heart pounding. I need to find Juliette, but if the fighting is happening this close to our territory, then she could well be involved. Either way, the enforcer has to be present--it would be criminal for someone of my position not to be with them.

I send a text to Tank to go after Juliette and message me at the first word. After that, I muster the men, and within half an hour, every engine that could be spared for the Heartbreakers is rumbling outside the clubhouse.

"Listen up!" Breaker barks from his own motor-cycle, riding slowly up and down the lineup of gleaming black motorcycles and Heartbreaker colors on our kuttes. "We've got a report from the border of our territory! Buzzsaws shot at our scouts, they shot back, and they chased them east until the Buzz-saws brought in reinforcements--and we're gonna go show them what happens when they try to slide up into Heartbreaker country!"

A baritone cheer goes up in our army, and I give the signal to fall into formation as I ride ahead of the rest along with the other four officers.

We're going to war.

I feel so raw and exposed, like all the combined years of anxious nightmares about being naked and vulnerable in public have conglomerated into one big living terror. It's strange, coming back to this town yet again. It feels like I'm always fighting to escape it and no matter what method of transportation or what kind or company I keep, this place always manages to dig in its claws and drag me right back. There are all these different little colloquialisms and sayings about this town, about how hard it is to go and stay gone. About how there's some kind of silent curse that wraps around and holds you even when you think you're free. No matter how you leave, by plane or car or foot-to-gravel, this town is sticky. You might think you've shaken it loose, you're all clean. Home free and free from a place that begs you to call it home. But it doesn't matter how sweet that so-called freedom tastes. Everyone comes back. For familial obligations, for nostalgia, for familiarity. And sometimes, maybe even most of the time, because the big whirling world beyond the city limits isn't made for people like us.

It almost makes me laugh to think about how naive I was when I first left Wyoming and moved off to the big city. I was barely more than a child, though of course I didn't see a child when I looked in the mirror. I saw a young woman who had already endured enough suffering to push my psychological age a little higher. A little older. I was coming out the other side of a dark tunnel, of that I was convinced. I had stars in my eyes and the winds of change lifting me off the ground and blowing me across state lines. But the winds of fortune didn't blow my way. I doubt they ever will. Girls like me, we have to make our own fortune. We have to brew up our own good luck. Sometimes that means we have to grind against the grain, double back on the path we have wandered so hopelessly far along. But no matter how much time has passed and how lost I got in the meantime, I can always find my way back home. It's in me, preprogrammed into my internal compass.

Wyoming is my due north and always has been, but these days, the compass is spinning wild. It doesn't take a map to follow the reasons why.

I feel like my heart is being tugged in multiple directions, like the center of my universe is yo-yo'ing back and forth across state lines and across the sprawling plains of Wyoming. On the one side, there is the one person I have always run to, not even for my own comfort, just because I knew nowhere else to run. My mother. The one who raised me, who did her very best even if sometimes it probably wasn't quite enough.

The world certainly didn't do much to make her already-difficult job any easier. I may not be a mother myself, but I have no illusions about the complexity and weight of motherhood. Especially when money is tight and bad news seems to follow you everywhere you go. Each corner we turned, there was something new to confront. Bills to pay, services being turned off. The power going out in the middle of the night, plunging the halls of my childhood home into pure darkness and silence. I remember being terrified one of those nights in particular. I woke up in the middle of a fitful night-mare, tangled up in the sheets and sweating, only to find the house utterly still. I remember reaching for the bedside lamp and tugging vainly on the cord to turn it on. There was nothing I could do to bring back the light, no matter how many times I pulled the cord. The lightbulb didn't respond.

Nobody was coming to fix the problem. There was no tall, dark hero on his way to bring back the light. The darkness hung around my bed like a canopy of despair. I remember so distinctly the moment of clarity that hit me, when I realized that no matter how "good" I was, how well I behaved, how much I sacrificed to make things better or easier for my family, I couldn't fix it all. Not by myself. I had no money, no means, and no authority. That feeling of having absolutely no control over my surroundings has stayed with me even throughout the years. I suppose you could call it a compulsion. I keep trying to put things back together, but damn, they just fall apart so quickly. All I want is for all the pieces to fit like they should. Not perfect but still holding. A mosaic in every color. A hue for every pain and joy and fear and relief. Shapes to represent every looming figure in my universe.

My mother would certainly be the largest figure in the stained glass image. That's why I had to do it. I had to betray the man who would call me wife. He asked me to trust him, and there's a huge part of me that wants to, that already does. But I can't just shrug off my responsibilities so easily, just because he looks better-equipped the carry the weight. That scenario isn't fair to anybody involved, and besides, I know better than to let myself rely on anyone but me. Maybe that makes me paranoid or whatever. Oh well. I have to do this.

I have to be cautious about it, though. I know what's at stake here. So I don't pull right up to my mother's house. I park a couple blocks down the street and sit there for a few moments with the engine still and my breaths coming deep and slow. I look around the painfully familiar neighborhood, scanning for signs of trouble. An overly nosy neighbor. A shifty-looking pedestrian. Kids on their bikes. But all is quiet. I can hear nothing beyond my own breaths and the faint wistful wind outside. I close my eyes for a second. I don't even have to look to know where to go. After all, these are my old stomping grounds. I remember the lay of the land. I can keep to the bushes and the overgrown hedges as I make my way down the street. If I do it right, I can get to my house without anyone noticing me. That would be ideal. I'm already going to be in a heap of trouble with Big Daddy, but I don't want to make it worse.

I quietly open the car door and slip out onto the street. My feet don't make a single sound as I pad up into the grass line of the nearest yard. I'm grateful for the lack of traffic and activity on the streets of my neighborhood. It dawns on me that I'm not entirely sure what day it is. Maybe everyone is at work. Maybe everyone is sleeping in. Who knows? Either way I just don't want to be noticed. I try to keep my head down and be as unobtrusive as possible. I have to get to my mother's house without being detected. For all I know, Big Daddy could have eyes and ears out everywhere, trying to hunt me down already. My heart does a sad little split. It hurts to even think about him. My husband. My savior and captor at the same time. I should fear him, but the pull and ache of my soul tells me there's more than fear making me feel sick to my stomach. I feel guilty. I feel like I've turned my back on someone important.

It's hard to sort out what I am supposed to be feeling right now. My emotions are a hailstorm of chaos. And I doubt it will get any less chaotic once I get to my childhood home. But I have a duty to accomplish, damn the consequences. I move up closer and closer, feeling my heart race ever faster as my childhood home looms before me. Something about it sends a shiver down my spine. I wonder instinctively if it has something to do with whoever may be inside-- apart from my mother, anyway. After all, if Daddy is to be believed, then there's someone appointed here to look over her. The one named Tank, if I recall correctly.

Whoever it is, I'm going to plow right through him. Even if he *is* a tank.

I slither along the side of my house. I know all the different ways, both intended and improvised, to get into this house, and it does not necessarily involve a door. I shimmy through the bushes under the window and reach out to open the back gate. It looks for all the world like it's securely locked. I'm sure the guy stationed here thinks so. But he doesn't know the secrets this house holds. I smile to myself as I jostle the lock just ever so particularly in that way it needs to fall open. That gives me a little rush of confidence. I'm on my own turf. As harrowing as it can be to defy Big Daddy, it does feel oddly invigorating to be back in my old stomping grounds. I slink into the backyard, keeping close to the wall as I work my way up the back patio staircase. After a childhood of walking on eggshells, I know how to keep my head down. I know how to shape my every step for minimum sound and impact. If I don't want to be detected, I fly under the radar. It's a skill I think every kid who grows up under some degree of fear has to cultivate in order to survive. We know how to avoid trouble… although some of us seem destined for trouble despite our best efforts.

I thought I could outrun my trouble. Put miles and years between it and me.

Valiant effort on my part, but foolish. Overly optimistic. I move slowly down along the wall, my feet padding silently across the wood planks. The sliding glass door is my new obstacle. The thick white blinds are drawn, but narrowed. Leaving thick wedges of exposed glass, a potentially clear view straight through to me, if anyone happens to be sitting in the den. That's just a risk I have to take. I take a deep breath and dart to the door, crouching down and swiping the toe of my shoe under the scuffed-up, frayed side of the rug at the doorway, sweeping a rusty old hair pin out, stuck to some sappy pine needles. I don't even take a beat to look up and see if anyone is watching me. It's now or never. The adrenaline is pumping through my veins and I take my chance. I swipe the key from the ground and jam it into the door lock. I give it a frenzied twist and the old, crusty lock snaps perfectly open. I don't pause to question what I'm doing. There isn't time for that. I have to think on my feet. If someone happens to be in there watching my every move, waiting for me to step through the doorway and right into their grasp... then I will cross that bridge when I reach it. With my heart racing, I finagle the lock open and I pull hard on the latch. Moment of truth. The door makes a low whooshing noise as I yank it open.

Without another second of hesitation, I slip inside and close the door shut behind me, my eyes wide and gazing out through the dimly-lit den. The blinds are drawn enough to keep the room in relative darkness, even though it's daytime. I wonder if that has something to do with the guy stationed here. Maybe he likes to maintain a base level of unease by keeping the lights low. Or maybe it's a tactical choice, to protect my mother by giving troublemakers the impression that nobody is home. To put them off the scent. Who knows? Either way, I'm just relieved to not see anyone right away. I listen, standing stock still in the den. I close my eyes and strain to pick up any noise in the house. At first, I don't hear anything. And then a familiar voice echoes softly through the house and I go rigid. Until it dawns on me who the voice belongs.

Alex Trebek. My mother is watching Jeopardy. I can't help but smile. Of course, she is.

My heart lurches with affection and longing for my mother. It's probably the tiny childhood version of myself still kicking around in the back of my mind. On top of that, there's my duty to protect. My instinct to keep the few souls I care about safe from harm. I need to see her with my own eyes. Only then will I be able to relax. I have to know Big Daddy keeps his word. So I creep through the den and make my way up the stairs, listening to the volume of my mother's television rise louder and louder as I approach. I pause at the mouth of the stairs, peering down the darkened hallway. I let my eyes adjust to the dimness and once I'm certain there's nobody lurking down the hall, I start making my way down to the door I know belongs to Mom's room. To my surprise, the door isn't locked. In fact, it's not even fully shut. I can see a tiny shaft of glowy television light through the doorway. My heart races even faster. Could it really be this easy? It seems impossible, or at least unlikely. Nothing about my life has been simple lately, so finding my mom unguarded and accessible without having to put up a fight or outfox some big burly guy... it feels like a trick.

But I swallow back that swell of paranoia. I dart

across the hallway, inching closer to the bedroom door as my heart thuds painfully in my ribcage. I don't quite know what to expect inside the room. That is, until I hear my mother mutter under her breath.

"Oh, that was an easy one. How'd nobody get that?"

I can barely hold back a laugh as I knock gently at the partly-opened door. My mom startles out loud. I can just picture her clasping a hand to her chest, eyes wide and hair wild at all angles. Suddenly, I want to hug her with the deepest pull of my heart. But I have to proceed with caution. The last thing I need is to give my mom a panic attack.

"Who's there? Tank? That you?" she calls out.

"Wrong answer," I reply, stepping into the doorway.

My heart swells when the look on her face transforms from concern to pure elation.

"Oh, my sweet girl!" she says happily. "It's good to see your face. Come in!"

I hurry to her bedside and perch on the mattress, beaming. She looks surprisingly healthy and well-rested, the perpetual circles under her eyes slightly less shadowy than usual. The laugh lines on her face stand out more than the frown lines, maybe. In this light. For just a moment.

"How are you doing? Are you alright?" I ask her with genuine concern.

She smiles softly. "Yes, honey. I'm fine. Quite well, actually."

"Really?" I press. I can't help but be suspicious.

"Oh yes. My caretaker has been doing a wonderful job of keeping me, you know, alive," she laughs. "He may look like a big, burly tough guy, but I swear he's a real softie."

Can she really be talking about Tank? I guess he has a different side to him than I've seen. I reach across the bed and put my hands over hers, looking into her eyes for any sign of deception. I want to know if she's telling the truth or just cushioning the reality of her situation to make me feel less worried. After all, she is my mom. She wants me to be happy. She doesn't want to weigh me down with the burden of her safety and wellbeing, although I have willingly shouldered that exact weight ever since I moved back home. It's hard to let go of that heavy responsibility, hard to let someone else, some guy I don't really even know, take care of arguably the most important person in my life: Mom. But I can see in her eyes that she's genuinely okay. In fact, the only thing wrong is that she appears to be more concerned about me.

She sighs, peering into my face. "Sweet girl, I cannot even pretend to know what all is going on in your world right now. You have to forgive me if my memory is a little sparse. Sometimes it's a little confusing..."

I nod, quick to assure her. "It's okay. You don't have to understand. I don't think I could properly explain what's been going on even if I wanted to," I admit.

"Are you safe?" she asks.

I swallow hard and force a smile. "Yes. I'm safe."

"Well, then, that's the best a mother can hope for, right?" she says cheerily. Then her face falls a little. "Of course, I wish I could say the same about my other child."

My heart stumbles over a beat. Diesel.

"Have you heard from him at all?" I ask her, trying to keep my tone casual. I don't want to tip her off that there's a massive war at hand.

"No. You know how he likes his freedom and his privacy. The more I reach for him, the farther he pulls away," she laments, shaking her head. "That unexpected visit he paid us a while back was the first time I've seen him in months. You know the kind of gang he runs around town with. Not very nice boys."

"That's an understatement," I grumble.

"It's just... those motorcycles. I swear they addle your brain or something. I wish I knew how to bring him back," Mom murmurs. "I try not to overthink it and get all worked up, but I have to admit I worry about him. I just know he's fallen into some bad stuff. It's embarrassing to say, but I've stopped looking for bikers in the news. I just... I don't want to know."

I nod slowly. "I can understand that."

She pats my hand with her own trembling one. "You always do, darling. I can count on my sweet girl. I just wish I knew how to get your brother's mail to him. I have a forwarding address, but that caretaker keeps telling me not to get involved. Very frustrating."

My heart pounds. "You have a forwarding address for Diesel?" I mumble.

She cocks her head to one side. "Diesel?"

"Don't worry about it. Uh, could you write down that address for me?" I ask innocently.

"Yes, of course," she says, picking up her ever-present little notepad filled with checklists and reminders. She scribbles down the address, rips out the little page, and hands it to me.

I hop up, tucking the paper into my back pocket. Mom looks startled. A little disappointed, too. I can tell she was hoping for a longer visit with me. It breaks my heart to leave her, but I know the risks. I'm on the lam. I don't have time to waste.

"You going out again?" Mom asks wearily.

"Yes. But don't you worry about me, okay? Relax. Focus on yourself," I urge her.

"I'll do my best," she answers. "Come back soon, please. And if you go visit your brother, can you take him his mail and tell him Mom says hi?"

I know I can't fulfill her requests. But she needs me to lie. So I lie.

"Yep. Will do," I answer hastily. "Bye, Mom. Love you."

"Love you, too!" she calls out after me.

My brain is firing in all directions as I race downstairs and out to the street. I hurry back to my car and hop in, relying on my knowledge of the town's layout to find my way to the address on the sheet of notepad paper.

As I drive, getting closer and closer, I wrack my brain for the best approach. I need to confront my brother. He needs to know that his actions have consequences, that his little gang is causing big problems. I need to ask him those difficult questions. I need to know what the exact fuck he's been doing all this time. My own brother has become an enemy, at least in the eyes of the man who saved me. So much has happened. So much has changed-- not the least of all, me. It's hard to say where my allegiance should lie. I can't help but lurch toward Daddy. His strong arms and steady gaze, his hoarse growl pronouncing my name like a magical incantation in my ear. My body reaches for his in the moral darkness, again and again.

But visiting my mom has brought me back, in a way. These familiar streets. The way the sun arches beams of golden light through the trees so that their shadows cast long and jagged across the back roads I rumble down. I think to myself, I've been here before. But then, I've been everywhere in this town.

There are only so many paths to take. In my years of teenage boredom, I must have roamed every nook and cranny of the city limits. I can't recall street names, but the precise angle of the green sign leaning over the dewy grass is imprinted in my mind. I would recognize it anywhere. I don't need a GPS. I follow the instinctual, directional pull of memory, and it leads me to a rundown house in a gray, sleepy part of town.

A shiver of cool dread rolls down my spine. I can see the house number just a few mailboxes down. I double check it with the paper crumpled in my hand. I cut the engine and sit for a moment, just taking deep breaths. I watch the street closely, barely daring to blink and miss something vital. I need to get a feel for the place, iron out the vibes and know how big the risk I run really is. Anytime my brother is involved, it's a pretty sure guarantee trouble is close behind. The past is already closing in on me, but I can't let it drag me down. With one last surge of courage, I quietly open the car door and slip out onto the cracked sidewalk. I lock the door, pocket the keys, and start making my way down the street to the faded address. I turn down the driveway, storming for the door. I'm steeling myself up, getting lost in the arguments playing out in my head, when suddenly the air is pierced with a frightened squeal. I stumble back, looking up toward the sound. It's come from a window in Diesel's house. I can see through the tattered white blinds-- a pretty young woman, shrinking back and cowering from something much larger that looms over her. It doesn't take more than a millisecond for me to realize it's my brother.

The woman looks exhausted and browbeaten, like all the hope has been knocked out of her body. My brother is shouting at her, hurling insults and accusations by the sound of it. The words are garbled through the glass but I feel the poisonous tone leaking through. I know how sick she must feel right now, just desperate for the tirade to end. Poor girl. I assume she must be his girlfriend... or *one* of his girlfriends, that is. But there's no writing this off as a simple lover's quarrel when I see Diesel violently backhand the woman, a look of callous disregard on his face as she shrinks to the floor in shock. I gasp and clap a hand over my mouth, totally horrified.

Then, a white-hot rage flares up inside of me. I can't see him do that to another woman.

I dart up to the door and I barely have time to marvel at the unlocked handle before I burst into the house, wailing and flailing like a madwoman. Anger propels me across the room, moving so quickly that Diesel doesn't get a chance to stop me. I push past him, knocking him back. I don't give him a single glance as I rush toward the girl with the swollen pink cheek and offer her a hand. She looks into my eyes, hers wet with tears, and instinctively trusts me. I pull her up and all but shove her out the door.

"Go! Don't look back!" I cry out to her. She's hyperventilating and murmuring confused thank yous as she runs away.

I don't get an opportunity to watch her safely disappear, though. I can hear Diesel's heavy boots coming toward me. I hastily slam the door shut and dodge his attack. He slams into the door hard, grunting and growling fiercely.

"Where the hell did you come from?" he snarls.

"Same place you came from," I bite back.

"Oh, screw off!" he spits. "You and I have nothing in common."

"Thank god for that," I reply.

"Why are you here, Juliette? What do you want?" he groans.

"I want you to be honest for the first time in your life! I want you to tell me what the hell you've been doing all this time, messing around with that damn biker gang. Who are you? Who the fuck is Diesel and where did my brother go?" I hurl at him.

Before he can even respond, a big guy comes lumbering down the hallway toward us. Reinforcements. A bodyguard. Of course.

"What's going on in here?" he demands. "Diesel, what the hell? I just saw the girl running down the street through that back window!"

I dive for the door, even as it puts me dangerously closer to Diesel.

"Nobody is going after her! Let her go!" I hiss.

"I'll deal with you," the guy growls at me.

"Keep out of this, Chainlink!" Diesel barks at him.

Chainlink glowers angrily. "I'm not the one who needs to stay out of it!" he retorts, pointing at my hand.

It takes me a moment to realize what he's indicating.

Oh god.

My ring. Diesel's eyes widen and he pounces at me, yelling. "What did you do? It can't be true!" he snarls.

"Stay back!" I shout back, balling my hand into a fist.

Preparing to sock my brother in the jaw with the ring Daddy gave me.

That moment before the two sides clash feels like the calm before a storm wrapped into one. Before me is the plains on both sides of us, sprawling to one flank onward and onward until fences start to line the endless landscape beyond. On the other is a lonely old abandoned silo and a squat, decrepit building sitting just off to the side of it. The road doesn't have a driveway onto it so much as an extension of the road and dirt, and beyond the buildings are dry hills that ramp up into cliffs. Blue skies overhead. It's big sky country.

And right in front of us, barreling for us just as fast as we're charging toward them, are the Buzzsaws and as many engines as they could muster, with reinforcements roaring out from behind the silo.

The moment feels still. Someone on the other

side has a sawed-off shotgun raised, and as they draw closer, he and the rest of the gang drawing weapons are about to start firing off rounds. We're just a little closer to the abandoned gas station than they are, and that's the only advantage we're going to get in this scrap. Both sides are acting on a snap call to action. Neither of us has had more than a few minutes to plan, but neither side is willing to get driven out of its territory.

Small as they are, skirmishes send an important message. We don't want bodies, but if bodies are what it takes, then the Buzzsaws have already long since crossed that line with a lot of women's bodies. But this isn't just a skirmish, it's a skirmish at an outpost that is most definitely not as abandoned as the ragged old gas station looks, and that means it's got to go.

That's why I don't feel too bad when the first shot that leaves my gun hits a Buzzsaw enforcer in the shoulder and sends him spinning out, nearly taking out the guy behind him as the road bursts into a roar of gunfire.

Our bikes tear into the gas station and roar behind the building for as much cover as we can all grab in as little time as possible. We might not have had long to plan, but my plan's not a complicated one. It never is. Doesn't need to be.

In the hail of gunfire that hits the bricks around the front side of the building, I'm among the crowd hurdling to the back. There might be people we need to save inside that building, so the Heartbreakers are planning to push the fight as far away from it as we can.

But we still need someone on the inside to go poking around. That's where I come in.

As soon as I can come to a stop, Ironside does the same behind me, and two of our men dart ahead of us to take cover by a rusty dumpster, where we can hear the sounds of engines rolling up nearby. I don't have long to get out of sight. Ironside follows me as I barrel for the back door, and we cover each other as we break inside.

The door hits resistance immediately. Someone-- or more than one someone, by the sounds of things--was coming through the other side when I thrust the door in. I reached through and grabbed, feeling my fingers wrap around leather kutte, and that was all I needed to get a hold of. Ironside and I push the door open as I tackle my way in, throwing the man I'd grabbed to the ground while Ironside ran past me to take care of the second biker who's trying to get his gun out while going for the door to the rest of the gas station.

Ironside grabs him before he can make it out, and while I focus on my man, I know he's got his in hand. Before the guy in my arms can so much as get his bearings, I grab the back of his head and crack it to the ground, knocking him out cold. By the time I stand up, I see the man Ironside was fighting crumple to the ground, and Ironside presses himself against the wall and looks beyond the door while I do the same on the opposite side.

We get our guns out, but there's no need. The place seems empty, save for the rumbling and gunfire we can hear outside.

"They've definitely used this place as an outpost," I say after we do a sweep of the ruins. "I can tell where they were using the shelves for storage and left a few cots in the aisles."

"Let's make sure they didn't leave anyone behind," Ironside says. "It looks like they packed up."

"Why'd they have people out here waiting to defend a stale outpost?" I growl.

"If they packed up not long ago, then a place like this isn't a bad spot to set up a fight," Ironside said. "Especially if they want to get an idea of our numbers--and think they stand a chance of thinning them out."

"If they've already got one of those, let's make sure they don't get the second," I say as I get low and sweep the whole gas station.

It's not easy to search a place with a firefight happening outside, but there isn't much to search. There are no prisoners here, and Ironside is right. It looks like they only had a couple of people here watching out and waiting to start a fight to test our defenses, and that was what they'd gotten.

"Let's get back outside and disengage the men," Ironside grunts, and he darts out of the office I'm searching before I can reply. I run after him, but once we're outside, I we can see that the battle is already ending.

We see some bikes and bodies on the roadside, but there hasn't been much blood on either side, at a glance--and the crew retreating is hightailing it, so the theory that this was ground they meant to give might have held some water. I can't be sure, but I'm seeing the backs of Buzzsaws as some of our men break off to chase them away, and that's something I can't say I mind.

Something's not right, though, and just as I'm thinking that, I feel a buzzing in my pants. I reach in and look at my phone, because there are only a handful of people who could be calling me right now who aren't right here with me, and all of them would be emergencies.

Tank is not the name I'm expecting to see on caller ID.

"Tank, what's going on?" I say immediately. "We just ran off Buzzsaws from the site."

"Thank god, I called six damn times, thought they'd gotten you," he cackles. "You're not gonna believe this one, but I tracked him down."

"What?" I say, furrowing my brow and turning to stalk back toward the gas station. "Who?"

"Diesel!" he says with bloodthirsty cheer. "I

tracked Juliette and followed her to a house--and he's here. We can move in and take him down, he's away from his pack!"

"Don't you fucking do it," I say, my heart suddenly racing.

"What?!" Tank barks. "This is our chance, man."

"Not if it puts Juliette in danger, that was the whole fucking point of me going out of my way like this, Tank," I say in no uncertain terms. "No. Diesel is not above using her to defend himself."

"We can't just walk away from this, BD," Tank says. "This is bigger than us, if we keep letting Diesel keep his distance, we're never going to-"

"Meet me halfway," I interrupt him suddenly, looking back out to the group.

"What?"

"I'll text you a location, but start heading my way and I'll meet you there," I say. "If we take action, I'm not letting it happen without me there."

"Are you sure Breaker is gonna be down for that?" he asks.

"You let me worry about that," I grunt. "But I need to know you won't-"

"Fine, fine, I'll head your way," he says. "Don't get shot."

I hang up the phone, and I shake my head as I trudge over to meet Breaker, who's leaning on his bike handlebars as he stares out after the Buzzsaws making their escape, having hung back with the rest of the group. He turns and nods to me as I approach while the other men gather the wounded and making sure they're disarmed.

We're fighting for peace, not blood, if we can avoid it.

"Got news, Prez," I say as he turns to me. "And I'm going to level with you, but I'm going to tell you up front this isn't something I'll negotiate on."

"Let's hear it, then," he says, narrowing his eyes.

"Tank knows where Diesel is," I say, and Breaker's eyebrows go up. "He's away from the pack, and he's at his house. But Juliette's there, too, and I don't know why they're meeting. All I know is, I've got to get over there now and get her out of there before she gets hurt."

"Shit," he snarls, spitting on the ground. "You know we can't let him slip out that easy if we've got him, brother. Are you sure Tank's intel is good?"

"He says he's got eyes on them, but he's meeting me halfway back," I say. "With all due respect, this is personal--I'm not asking permission here, Prez."

"That so?" he says, nostrils flaring as the subtle challenge while he looks me up and down. "If time weren't a factor I'd be arguing more. Alright, here's what we'll do: you go on the condition that we back you up. I'll send the guys to chase the Buzzsaws clear of their boss, and we head him off and give you a chance for a little heart to heart."

I glare him down, knowing full well that I'm

under as much pressure to negotiate fast here as
he is.

"Fine," I say at last, giving him a curt nod."

"Good," he says, grinning. "Now, let's get the fuck
out of here and roll fast."

BIG DADDY

ank made good time, and we catch up with him at a gas station more than halfway to our side of the route. He's pissed when we show up for even going out of the way this far, but he's more eager to get back on the road and tear back down to Diesel before he gets away. I don't even care about him, if I'm being completely honest. I mean, I do, but not in the way the others do.

I'm going for Juliette. The guys know that. They couldn't stop me if any of them want to.

Riding with the original Heartbreakers fills me with a kind of peace. Breaker, Bones, Ironside, myself...and the new guy, but Tank's at least earned his stripes. There's no one thing about it. It's in the rush of the ride, the faith we have in each other, the sense of community, the smell of the road and gasoline, watching the sun sail overhead.

It's brief. I don't get to enjoy it for more than one short, hard ride that feels ten times longer than it is to me. All I can think about is Juliette, about feeling that warm, nimble body wrapping itself around me in bed while I run my hand up soft, bare thighs. Those kinds of thoughts keep me company on the ride, even if they make my pants a little less comfortable.

Tank gives us a gesture that we're not far from where we're headed, and I'm mildly surprised. It's a small town that's on the outskirts of Buzzsaw territory, not the kind of stronghold in the dead center that I was expecting. Then again, I supposed the best hiding spot for a safehouse was somewhere hidden and unsuspecting.

I respect all of our members, but I have a hard time imagining us stumbling on this place if we went looking for it on our own. My hands dig into my handlebars, feeling burning anger in my blood. Juliette's connection to Diesel is turning out to be what might kill him...and I don't know if Juliette will forgive me for that, regardless of how things play out here.

There's a fucking lot going on and I need a fucking minute to stop and think about things, and I don't have that. Hell, I haven't had time to stop and do anything, much less the one thing I want to do. My anger just builds as we ride, peace melting away to rage the more I think about how much of a bullshit no-win situation Diesel has set us up for.

Frankly, I want to put a bullet between his teeth for it all. But what happens when the three of us are in a room together is for me to find out.

Our ride takes us through a little trucker town off an interstate exit. There's not much to it besides a motel and a handful of the usual fast food and gas stop businesses, and I happen to know it's not the best area--rough around the edges in the way we tended to watch out for.

Once we're past it, though, we're only on the road for a few more minutes before all of us spot the same thing ahead of us around the same time. Tank looks back at us as if to confirm that he and Breaker aren't seeing things, but we most definitely do.

It's a woman, and she's staggering up the side of the road.

There's obviously something wrong with the way she's walking. As we get closer, I can tell that she's unwell, her clothes are tattered, and she has an arm feebly extended to the road with a thumb up.

As soon as we're close enough that she can see us, though, and she registers what's hurdling toward her, she turns and tries to run away from the road. She must have seen the bikes and taken off running. She would have no reason to run from Heart-breakers if she knew who we were. That gives me a good idea of what she's really running from.

We pull over to the side of the road and cut her off before she can get far, and Tank moves around into her direct path with a hand out and a "Woah, woah, easy, we're on your side!" assurance that the girl doesn't seem convinced of as she looks around.

"I'm not going back!" she snaps immediately, trembling despite looking malnourished as hell and about to fall over from exhaustion.

"Nobody's taking you back anywhere unless it's somewhere you want to go," Tank says in as soothing a tone as a man like him can manage.

"Where did you come from?" I ask.

"Who are you?" she asks, showing remarkable bravery all things considered.

"We're the Heartbreakers," Tank says. "We help out folks who look like they've had a rough day. You look like you've had a rough day. I've got a blanket and some water in my hutch, if you want to take a breather," he says, carefully dismounting his bike and standing invitingly for her.

She cautiously looks at all of us, then steps forward toward Tank. "Cindi," she says at last. "My name's Cindi Barrows."

"You're one of the girls who's been in the news recently," Breaker remarks, nodding. "I thought your face looked familiar."

"People are looking for me?" she asks with wide eyes. "I-I've been with these bikers who...this woman came and sent me out out of nowhere, I didn't even get her name, but-"

"Wait, slow down, one thing at a time," Tank says.

"We know what those men were going to do with you," I say, giving her a grim nod. "But you don't have to worry about that anymore, we're going to put an end to that."

"I came from a house," she breathes. "It's off Canyon Road just half a mile or...or something, I-I'm not sure."

"I know where that is," I say, nodding. "Don't worry, sounds like we're headed to make sure nobody comes after you."

"Are...are you serious?" she says breathlessly.

"Will you come with me?" Tank asks. "I'll get you to our clubhouse where you'll be safe, unless you've got somewhere to go. You look like you could use some food, first of all."

She nods almost immediately, then gives the rest of us a wary but grateful look, smiles, and gets on the bike with Tank to tear off down the road.

And now there's nothing between us and Diesel...but Juliette.

My blood is still boiling, and there are little cut marks in my palm from where my fingernails dug in from clenching my fist so tight. My fingernails aren't even that long, it was just all I could do to keep from leaving a mark on Diesel's face for the things we fought about.

And we have not stopped.

"I don't want to hear it!" I shout at him as I turn and storm across the living room, grabbing my purse and feeling my legs shaking with anger in every step. "Just- just *stop!*"

"Yeah I *bet* you don't want to hear it!" he barks at me, and by now, Jesus Christ his voice is like a nail he's tapping into my skull with every syllable.

I can't be in here anymore, I can't.

"You never wanted to hear it!" he shouts, red-faced while I fumble with the door handle, feeling like an idiot who can't even manage a fucking *lock* while my own brother barks at me like he always has. "That's why you're about to run off again, aren't you? Good fucking riddance, you should have stayed gone the first time and not caused all this bullshit!"

I catch those words just as I'm stepping out the front door. It's not just the words themselves that sting like a scorpion stinger right into raw skin.

It's the *sincerity*.

I can usually tell when my brother is just being a shithead to be a shithead. It's something about his tone that gives it away. This is different. I can tell I've cost him real money, which is all he's ever cared about anyway. No wonder this is the only thing that gets an honest rise out of him is something that threatens his fucked-up income.

My skin is crawling. I just...can't stomach this right now. I slam the door behind me, fuming as I make my way to my car, and by the time I sit down in it and let my head thump back against the seat, I feel it all boiling over again. I slam the car door shut, cover my mouth with my arm, and scream.

I did this a lot when we were growing up. Back then it was a little slope by a reservoir I'd sulk off to and do the same thing, but the second I got a car, that became my sanctuary. It isn't much of one now that I'm a little more jaded than that, but the long, hard scream I belt out into the crook of my arm is still pretty satisfying. I scream until my throat feels sore, and then I let my head fall back onto the seat again and glare at the ceiling, feeling my heart racing.

Fuck him. Maybe he's right. I don't even know, I just want to get the fuck out of here and drive as far away as I can. I finally look up and adjust the rear-view mirror, and my heart promptly stops in its tracks.

Bikes.

There are motorcycles lined up out front, idling, all the riders staring at me as they block the drive-way. My eyes dart right to the one in the dead-center, the silhouette I recognize that makes my heart freeze for a beat. The next instant, I nearly jump out of the car to walk toward the row of bikers I recognize--all four of them, Big Daddy's bike gleaming black in the sunlight as he holds my gaze with an iron grip.

We glare at each other hard for a few long moments before I can't hold back anymore. I storm forward, and before he can even open his mouth to say something to him, I throw my arms around him just as he catches me.

I bite back tears as I dig my fingers into his kutte and breathe in the leathery, dusty scent that fills my nostrils as I lean against him, a mountain of steel that holds me comfortingly. His hands are rough, and he doesn't say a word, but he's as gentle as ever. I could melt into him, but I can't let myself be that vulnerable right now.

"I've missed you so fucking much," I breathe.

"You have no idea," he growls, hugging me tight.

I pull back from him and look around at the group, double-checking which ones are present. "One of you tailed me, didn't you?"

"Tank wouldn't apologize if he were here," Breaker says matter-of-factly.

"I gave you all the space I could," Big Daddy says, and I look up to him and into those dark eyes. "But we both know this storm is closing in on us whether we like it or not."

"I know what I saw in there," I say in a muted tone, lowering my eyes.

"We did too," Bones speaks up. "I'm guessing you're the one who sent her running out of this place?"

"Tank is taking care of her," Big Daddy assures me. "As for you, I need to get you out of here."

"Hell no," I say firmly. "I've got to go back in there."

"Hell no," he repeats, furrowing his brow. "You've seen what he can do when he's angry. He'll do worse."

"This is a family ordeal," I insist, not willing to budge on this.

"And you're my family now," he says in a tone that hits me like a bucket of fresh water I desperately need, bringing me such a soothing feeling that I didn't know I needed. "Not just because you're my wife, either," he adds with a wink. "That does make the rest of them family, too," he says with a jab of his thumb back to the rest of the Heartbreakers.

They give nods, and my eyes pan over each of them before coming back to Big Daddy.

"Is that how you're gonna make it be?" I ask with a soft smirk, crossing my arms.

"That's the way it's gonna be, 'cause I'm sure as hell not letting you walk back in there alone," Big Daddy replies without missing a beat.

Neither of us can speak for a moment, both of us glaring stubbornly at the other while I feel my heels practically digging into the concrete.

But then I remember the feeling of relief that swept me up when I saw him just a few minutes ago, and the same feeling I had when I was resting against his back on a bike or on his chest at night.

Those memories are some of the only smiles I've had in a long time. Now that guy has brought a whole entourage to the doorstep right at a time that I need it most. That's more than any blood relations ever did for me, and a hell of a lot more than any man has ever done.

Every instinct in me wants to fight it. I want to tell him to fuck off and turn right around to stomp in and go right back at screaming at my brother again. Big Daddy would probably still be here to catch me when I came out to scream a second time.

It's still all too fresh and too real that Diesel's bullshit runs so much deeper than I thought. But if there's one thing my *husband* has proven, it's that he's there to catch me when I'm at my lowest, and I can trust him when I'm in that place. I can't trust *anyone* when I'm in that place, and I never thought I would.

"Alright," I say, nodding. "Just you. I know the rest of you want to kill him," I say bluntly, looking around at the others, even though Bones tries to look innocent. "I don't want you to do that, but at the same time, I...I don't even know who he is anymore. And I don't know if the man in there can be saved. He isn't worth it, but he's not stupid. Maybe we can get out of here without-"

I trail off as I notice Ironside glaring down the road at the sound that I hear too. "Bikes," Ironside reports, and my heart drops.

"Your men?" I ask hopefully.

"None of them should be out here," Big Daddy says, dismounting his bike immediately and putting an arm around me as he looks toward the road and starts to tug me toward the house. "We need to get inside, that's probably Diesel's search squad he has looking for the girl who escaped."

"That means it won't be more than a handful of them," Bones says cheerfully, holding up a crowbar and brandishing it. "We'll keep them off your back, you two go have a chat."

"Those fuckers aren't going to be prospects," Big Daddy warns them as he walks toward the house with me.

"Yeah, these are men who ride with Diesel," Breaker says, rolling his shoulders back. "Look sharp."

The other three ride off just as I see more riders appear around the corner of the road, and one of them has a chain swinging from the side of his bike as they take notice. I feel Big Daddy squeeze my hand as we pick up our pace and break into a run, darting to the side of the house and keeping low.

Chainlink is leading the pack.

"Shit!" I hiss as I hear gunfire out front.

"I wasn't expecting a warm welcome," Big Daddy growls as we hustle. "Is anyone in there with Diesel that you know of?"

"No," I say quickly.

We make it around to the backside of the house, and I hurry to the door ahead of Big Daddy. Before he can reach me, I turn the knob and thrust the door open, just in time to hear the sound of a shotgun cocking.

BANG.

BIG DADDY

Cheap wood splinters in a dozen different directions as the shotgun shells annihilate the cabinets Juliette almost darted in front of. I hold her tight against me and feel shrapnel sting into my exposed shoulders, blood trickling down my tattoos as I shield her with my body. I grabbed her the second she got the door open, because I knew Diesel would be setting up somewhere in the house as soon as he heard two sets of engines pulling up.

He's a bastard, but he's a clever bastard.

I didn't come back here planning to put Diesel down, but it looks like he might not give me a choice. If he's opening fire on Juliette, then the quickest way to make that stop is to open fire on him, and she's going to have to understand that.

My pistol is out before I even think about letting Juliette go. I push her away from the doorway and fire a warning shot in that hits the wall and ricochets to the side, and I hear a curse from the opposite direction. Heavy footsteps head into the living room, and I take the chance to dart inside the kitchen and gain ground before Diesel can take it back. The only problem is, he's got a shotgun, and I've got a pistol.

Well, two pistols, I decide as I take out the second one strapped to my side and hold both out and at the ready. I waste no time, partly because I know Diesel won't give me any, and partly because I know another relative with every bit of Diesel's determination is about to come charging in behind me.

I learned my lesson the hard way about trying to shake her *or* keep her tied down.

Almost immediately, I see the glint of the shotgun coming around the corner, and I slam the door shut behind me to delay Juliette just a little longer as I dive out of the way to the kitchen floor. There's another hail of splinters as the shotgun destroys more of the cabinets--he doesn't want to make it an incomplete demo job, I guess.

The shotgun disappears from view, and there's one other entrance to the kitchen around the opposite corner. I start to run for it, but suddenly, a blast of drywall comes flying just in front of me as Diesel fires off a round *through* the wall with that heavy shotgun.

"Gonna be hard to get the insurance claim on this one, fuckhead," I growl as I take cover behind the stove, aiming my weapon around the corner of the metal.

"Whatever you leave your widow when I kill you will cover that bill," I hear him snarl from the far entrance to the kitchen just before the shotgun appears around the corner again.

As it does, there's a sudden *smash* as a cinderblock comes flying through the kitchen window nearest Diesel. Shards of glass fly everywhere, and I hear Diesel curse just before he fires into the ceiling and takes out the kitchen lights with a deafening pop. I catch a glimpse of Juliette ducking away from the shattered window as I take her distraction to race to the living room and pop around the corner with both guns out.

For a fraction of a second, I have Diesel down the sights of one of the pistols, and I'm ready to take the shot. As the tip of my finger slides over the trigger, the front door bursts open from the force of a hard kick that nearly knocks it off its hinges.

Both Diesel and I are stunned as Chainlink bursts into the room with a lead pipe in hand, blood on his face from outside and a wild look in his eyes as he barrels toward me without so much as breaking his momentum.

I fire a round at him that grazes a thigh before I have over six feet of him on top of me, and I'm barely able to roll with his swing to avoid taking the brunt of a lead pipe to the shoulder. We roll and topple together in a grapple, and I know I've got to be off this guy and on my feet in an instant if I want to make it out of here alive. Diesel probably isn't above shooting his own men if he can get away with it, especially if it means dealing with me.

I'm not going to give him the chance.

The second I get a free hand, still holding a pistol in each, I bring one down against Chainlink's head and hear a crack as he howls in pain. I push him off me and scramble to my feet just in time to see Diesel coming around the corner with that damn shotgun again. Not sparing a second, I fire from the hip.

"Fucking cock!" Diesel roars as he snatches a hand back to him, holding it to his chest as his eyes go wide while blood spills from it. At the same time, his shotgun falls from his hands...along with the trigger and middle finger I just shot off.

He tries to fall back into the living room, but I'm not about to let him go so easy now that he's injured. Abandoning Chainlink, I make a run for Diesel as he disappears behind the wall into the living room. I'm nearly on top of him already when I round the corner, and I throw my arms around him from behind before I feel us go into freefall.

When we hit the ground, one of my guns goes off, and the television pops loudly as it fizzles and smokes out of the new hole in the spiderwebbing screen. Diesel rolls and tries to throw his head back to strike my nose, but I wrestle him around without falling for any of his tricks.

I want a gun to his head so that I have a hostage. I can hear the sounds of battle outside, clanging metal and bullets in the street. Police will be on their way soon, if they aren't all bought in this area. If not, more bikers will be here. Juliette is just outside, and there's no safe place for her.

As I grapple with Diesel, I realize I'm wrestling with the devil in the thick of my own worst nightmare. In a heart stopping moment, I realize that since I've left Chainlink, he could run out the back-- and right into Juliette!

He's trying to wrench one of the guns from my hands while I try to get the other to aim, but we're deadlocked. Finally, I know I've got to make a sacrifice. I can get my hand out of his arm if I don't have that gun he wants so badly. With a flick of my wrist, I hurl it across the living room and under the television's entertainment center.

Free, I pull away from the now bloodstained Diesel, whose knuckle wound is flowing free now, and with a fluid motion I train my other gun on him.

He freezes.

"Gotcha," I growl in a menacing tone.

And that very second, Chainlink appears around the corner calmly, holding two pistols out and out the ready on me. I freeze.

We're at a standoff.

I have a gun trained on Diesel, but Chainlink has one on me. If I fire, Chainlink fires. That would be a no-brainer risk to take for me on a normal day, but Juliette is out back. She's managed to stay out of the firefight. I can't let that go to waste by leaving her alone to face Chainlink with me injured or worse.

"Well well well," Chainlink says. "I gotta say I like this kind of meeting better than the fuckin' pub."

"You have shitty taste," I say slowly, not moving a muscle.

Diesel, on the other hand, is squirming and trying not to show it. There's hatred in his eyes, but he's clutching that hand as it loses more blood than a man ought to be losing. Not to mention, that's his right hand I maimed. Best case scenario, it'll be a long time before he can ride again, much less shoot.

Chainlink's eyes aren't just on me, either. I see them flit to Diesel more than once while we all let the situation sink in.

"Get out of here," Diesel croaks at me, his voice raspy and low. "You're outgunned. What's gonna happen now is you're gonna put that gun down between us, I'm gonna take it from you, and we're gonna get a nice paycheck out of your buddies back home for you."

"How sweet, you won't even kill me," I say in a dull tone.

"Well now, I wouldn't kill my own brother-in-law," he says in a tone dripping with sarcasm. "But I guess I *could* make sure I don't have to deal with nieces and nephews before setting up your ransom."

"Tough words for a man who looks like he'll need a hand getting up," I say with emphasis on the word *hand*.

"Eat shit," Diesel snaps, his face turning red. "Chainlink, pick a fuckin' kneecap and teach our friend a lesson."

"Sure thing, Prez," Chainlink says cheerfully.

Without missing a beat, he casually swings one of his guns over to aim at Diesel and fires.

Diesel's eyes go glassy as bullet rips through his skull, they roll back into his head, and his body goes limp on the ground, dead. He never had time to realize he'd been betrayed.

My jaw drops, but I still have another gun trained on me that hasn't budged. Chainlink's gaze hasn't even left me. He doesn't show a flicker of remorse as Diesel's body twitches, and I smell the stench of shit in the air.

"Three's a crowd," he says with a menacing smile.

"Want to tell me what that was?" I ask cautiously, not convinced I have another turncoat on my hands.

"Smart business move," Chainlink reports with a smile. "Because you killed Diesel in cold blood when he was willing to negotiate. You sick fuck. Now, you're my ticket out of here safely, since you fuckers are trigger shy around your own, and *then* we're gonna see what you're worth to Breaker. If the boys don't want me to tear you to pieces to make an example, that is," he adds with a bloodthirsty chuckle.

Thump.

Chainlink staggers forward with dazed eyes and a slack jaw as his arms swing wildly. Juliette is standing behind him with the shotgun clutched tight in her hands, eyes wide, having just brought the butt of it down on the back of Chainlink's head *hard*.

Chainlink starts to lift his pistol with a dumbfounded grunt, but I'm faster. There's a single gunshot, and Chainlink falls to the ground as I lower my pistol watching Juliette's wide eyes.

I rush forward immediately and meet her in a hug, turning her away from her brother's corpse and leading her back into the kitchen as I feel her fast, heavy breathing in my arms. She's in shock over what she's just seen, and she can't speak as I lead her to the back of the house.

"Hey, hey, stay with me," I whisper to her as I hold her in the kitchen, but it takes little time for her to start taking deep, careful breaths and turning her dark eyes up to me. She mouths silently a little, holding it together so stunningly well, but I finally see the anger welling up in her eyes.

"That fucking bastard," she says, shaking her head. "That bastard."

"Both of them got what they deserved," I tell her soothingly. "And honey, we just cut the head off the snake. And then some. If it weren't for you, I'd be dead."

She looks up at me, lips trembling as they form a smile despite how much we're trying to hold in... and finally, she can't. She sobs into my chest, and I hold her close...just as I hear the sound of footsteps coming through the front door.

Both of us freeze, even Juliette mid-sob, and I raise my pistol again.

We might have just cut off the head of the snake, but I don't know who just won *this* battle.

I reach for a kitchen knife nearby as I hear footsteps approaching, but Big Daddy already has his gun out and aimed. I don't care if Chainlink got up from the dead and comes charging in after us, I'm not about to let a thing come between me and Big Daddy after what just happened in this house.

"Don't shoot, we won!" I hear Bones's voice say, and I grin ear to ear as Big Daddy hugs me tight, and the men come striding inside to survey the damage.

I can barely keep up with the next few minutes, I'm so dazed. I know what's going on--the MC is taking stock. It looks like they won big here, judging by the bikes outside, but Big Daddy gets me out of the house in short order. I'm grateful for that.

Whoever Chainlink killed might not have been my brother, but it sure as hell looked like him.

I'm vaguely aware that Big Daddy has said something to Breaker, and I get the impression we've been given the leave to go. The faces are battered, but smiling. They did what they came here to do-- they won. We won.

It was hard to think of it outside the context of my brother, though. But then, I'd just think of the face of the woman who escaped today, and I start to multiply that face over, and over, and over again. By the time I'm walking across the lawn to Big Daddy's bike with him, I can't shake the sense that no matter whether I could call that man my brother, his death saved a lot of women's lives and avenged the ones he's already broken.

I feel that deep down in my gut. There's just a lot of noise in the way.

"You were brave," my husband says as he swings his leg onto the bike. "Brash, so don't ever do something like that again, but brave. Can't say I wouldn't have done the same thing."

"We're on the same wavelength," I point out in a muted tone with a sad smile.

"You did what needed to be done," I say. "And you don't have his blood on your hands. What happened to him was because of the life he led."

"No, I know that," I say, nodding and closing my eyes. "In fact, this...it feels kind of like closure. I think I should have buried him a long time ago already."

He gives me a soft, sincere smile through that hard face.

"Come on," Big Daddy says in that husky tone, offering me a hand onto his bike with him. "Let's ride. You don't have to talk for a while if you don't want to. I know a good stretch through the plains."

A lump swells in my throat, and I smile at him softly before taking his hand. I think about it for a moment, but I don't look back at the house.

There's nothing for me there anymore.

The road ahead is open and free, and with every mile that Big Daddy takes me, the more I feel the crust and grime of the day's emotional toll softening. It's like the wind smooths it out, and I wrap my arms around Big Daddy's torso lovingly as I breathe in the leather scent of his kutte.

The plains sprawl in every direction as we rocket across them way over the speed limit but nowhere near law enforcement. Out here, it's just open road and freedom. Damn it, I get the appeal of the biker's life. I hate that I *get* it...but I also love it.

It means being a part of Big Daddy's world, and realizing that we're feeling the same thing as we roll across the empty space on a couple of rubber wheels might not seem like much in the big picture, but it gives me a whole feeling I don't think I'm acquainted with yet.

I want to get to know it more with him.

Walking into Big Daddy's house with him feels like stepping into a dark, comforting dream.

He shuts the door behind us as I turn around and look at him, finally in peace and quiet, finally alone. I've never been somewhere at peace with Big Daddy that wasn't just the eye of the storm at best. I've never seen him at peace.

I've never seen him like this, as fresh as it is.

Maybe it was all the recent crying making this feel so raw. Fuck, I don't like to let myself get this sentimental, but I'm way past that when this guy is concerned. I can see his desire in the flare of his nostrils as he steps toward me. I take a few tottering steps back, feeling *freeingly* vulnerable in his shadow.

I feel his desire pulsing in the darkness as thick as the bulge swelling between his legs. I feel warm as he closes in on me, but I keep walking back, smiling faintly as I lead him into his own living room.

I'm anything but a guide when my thigh bumps the couch leg, and Big Daddy loom over me before slowly bringing his large, rough hands to my face to cup it. I breathe deeply in the still air and focus on nothing but the face looking down on me.

He's been my captor and my protector. Hell of a way to start a relationship, hell of a way to get married, but I don't know if I could have careened through the past few weeks with anyone else. I don't even want to think of what it would have been like riding it out alone. I think about the girl that got away and what might have happened to me.

But then there's this giant.

He holds me, and I let him draw me closer as I close my eyes and feel butterflies in my stomach at his touch. He turns my face up, and he strokes my lip as I feel color rising in my cheeks.

"I've never wanted to need someone," I say.

"You don't need me," he says with a faint smile.

"Oh, I think I do," I say as the lump rises in my throat again with a faint trace of a smile as my heart pounds for him. "I really do, right now. I...I think you're a good one," I say with a smile I can't hold back. "And I feel good needing you. I feel good wanting you. I feel good loving you," I breathe, blinking away tears.

His hands slide back to show more of my face in the dim light and look at me, and I can see the shimmer in his own glassy eyes. "For a hard woman, you make me feel something pretty goddamn soft," he says, making my heart do a somersault as I hold back a laugh. "And if that's not love, I don't know what is. I love you with all that's left of my heart, Juliette."

He brings his lips to mine, and I feel the stubble brush against my face as my heart pounds so fast I feel lightheaded. The absolute power in his hands is so stunning when I think about how delicately he can handle me.

I let those hands roam down my shoulders, taking their time and feeling their shape before sliding down to do the same to my ass. He moans the moment he feels that, and he starts to grope me more greedily, pushing me down onto the couch behind us.

Love. I just told a biker I loved him. It was funny that thought came to me just now, as I'm getting my clothes stripped off and feeling my skin peppered with kisses from the man I'd trust with my life. Hell, the man I *have* trusted with my life so many times over...whether I meant to or not.

The feeling of that thick bulge against my thigh electrifies me. Once my shirt is off, he grabs the bra and unhooks it like it's a minor annoyance in the way. I see the familiar light that flashes through his eyes when he looks at my breasts, and the warmth blossoming through my body makes me aware of how wet I've gotten.

There's a hand wandering around the edge of my pants, too, and that tells me he's about to be aware of that fact as well. His fingers slide dangerously close to my pussy, and just as I'm waiting for him to make contact, his other hand brushes against my breast and palms it hungrily.

"Fuck," I let out in a gasp as he gropes my breast and lets me feel how stiff and swollen my nipples have gotten. His thick fingers trace circles around my areola, and a thumb teases the tip of the nipple in such a way that I feel my whole body tingling with warmth as I writhe and squirm under him.

It only takes one wrong squirm to let his hand slide between my legs, and he gets a feel of how wet I am. The grin on his face is downright wicked, and in all the emotional release that today has been, the physical one seizes up and makes itself known under the surface when I see that look on his face.

He slides two fingers to my clit as he brings his face down to my breast, moving his hand away and revealing that swollen, tortured nipple for him to lick his lips at before closing his teeth around it. He's as delicate as an artist, barely touching me with those sharp teeth, and the feeling it torments me with makes me want to cry out.

I'm already panting, and he's barely touched me. I can't say that for long as he starts swirling his fingers around in a small circle, rolling them over my clit. I'm stunned by how close I feel myself already. I'm a bowstring pulled taut, and I want him to shoot me over the moon.

I feel smooth, warm tongue bathe my stiff nipple, and I let out a shuddering whimper that's dripping with near shame. This feels like a betrayal of some things about my past self. But I don't feel guilty for it on an existential level. If I do, it's just a piece of the thought soup scalding my mind while he stirs it with every swirl of his tongue.

I tilt my head back and forth as I try to squirm

away from him, but before I can come, he draws his hand away from both my breast and my clit.

I gasp in protest, eyes springing open. He chuckles and winks at me while bringing those two finger to his lips and licking them clean while using his other hand to get my pants open. He pulls them down to reveal my glistening lips, and he has a hungry rumble in his throat as he parts my legs and lowers his face to me.

He doesn't even tease me. That beast of a face of his buries itself into my pussy, and his nose brushes against my clit hard. I gasp as his hands hold my hips, fingers digging in to get their grip while he uses his nose to tease my already tortured clit. My legs tighten against the couch as he brings his face up to let that massive tongue sweep into me

It licks up the length of my pussy all the way to my clit, where it misses contact by fractions of an inch on the first pass. It leaves me so desperate and wanting that I push my hips up gently, pouting with a soft sigh. One of my hands goes to his head to stroke while the other pushes me up on the couch.

On the second stroke, his tongue brushes my clit, and I moan openly. He dives in, tongue swirling in ways his fingers never could as it envelops the needy button and pushes against it mercilessly. My pussy is on fire, and I need more. Subtle little waves of tension are spreading out through my groin and out through my lower abdomen, and every time he pushes against my clit, I feel him fanning me that much hotter.

It boils over in an almost sudden, surprising crest that takes me off guard and makes me writhe with a sharp cry as my body convulses and comes hard. I squeeze my thighs as hard as I can, but I can barely budge the grip he uses to hold my legs apart and ravish my pussy with attention.

He doesn't stop at any point. He keeps that steady motion going, relentless, torturing me through the orgasm until he feels me start to come down from it. Just then, he stands up and slides his belt off, pulling out a thick shaft that I've missed sorely.

There's something primal about the way he grabs me, pushes my thighs apart, and presses a hard and fierce kiss to my lips before he slides his cock against my lips and slips it straight into my pussy. I moan hard into the kiss, whimpering and squirming as I feel a glowing wholeness from inside that brings that tension back in a subtle yet powerfully different way.

I feel totally helpless in his hands, letting go of myself at last just long enough to feel that golden pressure swell up into a thick blossom inside me as he ruts and thrusts faster with every inch that he delves into me. Soon, he's fucking me up to the hilt, and his heavy balls are swinging under me. I can feel their weight in every buck, and I dig my nails into his back as my orgasm pushes its way through to the surface.

I let out a long cry as I feel him start to lose his rhythm and spill over into a crashing orgasm while mine crests like a tidal wave and smashes through my body at the very instant he plasters my depths with a thick, heavy load of seed that pours out in shots that have his mouth open and his face pained.

Pulse after pulse, I watch him as my blood burns and tingles through my whole body. The electric current that spreads out through everything so forcefully finally retreats, and I feel myself full of my Daddy, glowing.

My eyes flutter open, and I look up at the man I love.

"If you think that poor excuse for a wedding is going to cut it for my wife," he promises me. "You've got another thing coming."

"Let's do it," I say, feeling the excitement rush through my heart as he lowers his face to mine, peppering me with kisses while still in me, letting out the last few soft pulses of come as my dark savior rocks me in the stillness of the night.

A week passes by in a flash after that night I poured my heart out to the last person I'd ever expect. We've had a lot of business to clean up in the wake of Diesel's death...but we can already feel the relief in the air.

The town looks nice--nicer than it has in a long time. Maybe longer than I've ever seen it. I've never been prouder to roll down Main Street with the four of us rolling up toward what has become the fanciest venue in town--our clubhouse. Granted, that bar might not be high in Pine Haven, but the way things are shaping up, it won't be that way for long.

But it's home now, even if it didn't start out that way.

I ride with Breaker leading the pack and the rest of us more or less in even formation alongside and behind him, confidently taking our time on our way to a meeting with our old friend Mayor Hartley. He had finally agreed to play ball after the news spilled out about Diesel. We made a few friends with journalists who'd been poking around at the missing women's disappearances for a while.

They were more than happy to swap a truckload of intel in exchange for some damn good publicity in the media.

Words are more important than actions, though, and that's what we've been giving the people of Pine Haven since we set up shop here. We used to get uncertain looks when we blazed through town, but now, as we pass shopkeepers and pedestrians out on their daily business, we get a few supportive honks and nods. We're not the kind of MC that good people fear, we're an MC for the people. We're not here to leech off the town, we've moved in and built it up.

The fact that Mayor Hartley is meeting on our turf is proof enough of that.

We pull up at our clubhouse, which stands tall and proud now that we own the building and have had more than enough support and funds to keep the place in pristine condition. Prospects come from all over the state to see this place, and now, we'll be even more proud to show it off.

At least, the outside is pristine. Inside, it's the same old MC hangout that it always has been and always will be, so long as we have a say in it.

A few minutes later, I'm sitting not at the conference table in the back room, but at one of the booths in the speakeasy-style bar downstairs. Mayor Hartley sits across from me between Bones and Ironside, while I flank Breaker as we drink local beers in the open. Kate leans behind the bar, overseeing from a distance, even though this is hardly a formal meeting.

Well, the mayor is under the impression it is, but we know what this is about. He's here to clear the air now that it's clear who the winner is in this conflict.

"Now about these uh, Buzzsaws," the mayor says, still grimacing at having to use the MC names proper now that they've made headline news. "You say they're dealt with as in, cleaned up? Done?"

"If you read the report Ironside put together," Breaker says, wearing his tattered kutte with no sleeves, looking as formal as he does when he rides on the dusty roads. "You'll see that Diesel's MC had a pretty simple hierarchy. The big dogs are gone, and we made sure that if there are any pups left in the area, they were prospects who might be worth reforming."

"We're the largest MC in the state now," Bones says proudly. "If anyone wants to ride, they'll be hearing from us. And we have eyes and ears from border to border."

"That means you're about to see human trafficking in Wyoming plummet," I say confidently, assuring the uneasy look I see in his eyes. "That much we can say without a doubt."

"There are a few club owners who scurried off who'll need to come to justice," Ironside adds.

"With the witnesses we're gathering coming forward about what happened to them," Breaker says, meaning the now-free victims of Diesel's sick operation, "we'll be able to start rooting *them* out too and keep the state's entertainment businesses as clean as this bar."

"I can't say I know how to speak your language, but it's hard to argue with the results," Mayor Hartey says with a tight smile, looking over to the bar that Kate's pretending to clean while listening in. "And I help my friends. Your soldier problem is going away. I don't want to *begin* to tell you what kinds of strings I had to pull to make it happen, but he's being redeployed, and he's staying gone."

"And the money his senator daddy was threatening us with is safe," Breaker says, as much to the rest of us as to Mayor Hartley. "This county just busted the biggest human trafficking ring the state has ever seen. It would make you look like a grade-A fuckwad to pull money out of Pine Haven now, and that's one thing senators don't like doing unless they can get away with it."

"Not like you, Mayor Hartley," Bones adds with a wink to our resident politician, who just takes a long drink of his beer.

"Right," he says tersely. "Well, I have to admit I'm surprised to have gotten a report in writing," he says as he picks up the folder Ironside handed him, "but this does give me time to look things over. It sounds like you have things in hand better than I could have expected, to be quite honest," he admits.

"Pleasure working with you, Mr. Mayor," Breaker says, showing amazing self-restraint in holding back his smugness. "You're doing your voters a real favor here. From the sounds of things, they'll remember that at the polls next year."

"Yeah, yeah," he says with a soft chuckle as he stands up. "Pleasure's all mine. Keep it up, gentlemen."

The mayor left us alone, and we all exchanged growing smiles before raising our glasses to each other and clinking them with a laugh of triumph together. That was the last thorn in our side shipped overseas, and now…

"All we've got left is to fill a big ol' vacuum Diesel left," Breaker says, clapping his hands together. "And don't you know it, lucky for us, we've got more turn-coats turning up as prospects every day. Hell of a week."

"You ain't fuckin' kidding," Bones says, shaking his head. "At this rate, we'll have to open a branch across the state."

"Don't talk dirty to me like that in front of my

girl, Bones," Breaker grunts, and we all laugh, including Kate, despite herself.

"Alright, it's about time we gave ourselves a night off, so I'm calling it here," Breaker says, standing up and smiling around at all of us. "We've done good work, boys. I remember sitting around a very different table with you all a long time ago when we got our reason to split from the Buzzsaws. We drew our line in the sand. Back then, one wrong move would have gotten us all killed."

"A few wrong moves almost got us all killed a few times," Bones adds, and I kick him under the table to another subtle round of laughter.

"All I've got to say is," Breaker says, smiling warmly at us all, "I'd stage a coup all over again with you crusty bastards."

We raise our glasses to that, cheering heartily, and we drink to comradery and good times yet to come before we take our leave. Breaker stays behind with Kate while the rest of us go upstairs, and once we're out, it was time to split for the night.

We'd have a celebration and then some on the way. Right now, we all need a little personal time to ourselves...and to our lovers.

And I have to go see my wife.

I feel like the grime of my past is washing off me in the hot shower. My hair is completely soaked, and the black tendrils snake down my shoulders and over my chest while I stand with my face directly in the stream, feeling the pressure batter my cheeks before I step back and take a breath.

This is life. I don't know exactly when the feeling hit me, but somewhere in this past week of the aftermath of the fight at Diesel's house, this transitioned into my new normal, or at least got a solid foot in the door. Showering in Big Daddy's shower feels like being home, in my safe place. And it's in part because I know he's on his way home.

I hear the bathroom door open, and I get goosebumps before I even turn around.

"Fuck," he groans at the sight of my silhouette

through the glass, and my heart races as I look over my shoulder at the misty outline of his figure approaching me through the fog. I run a hot shower, and the room traps it too much, which makes for an impressive effect as my giant of a husband steps through the mist and into view. "Looks like I have good timing."

He puts a hand to the glass and pulls it aside to peer in, and I lick my lips as I bat my dripping eyelashes at him. Big Daddy--or Big Hubby, like I tried to call him sometimes to his chagrin--strips his kutte off and hangs it on the door before stripping away the black tank top underneath and kicking his boots off.

"Looks like you had a good meeting, too," I say as he lets his pants drop, and I swallow at the sight of the already half-mast cock hanging between his legs. "And a good ride home."

"How'd you know I was thinking of you the whole way?" he asks as he steps forward, dusty body getting moist even before he steps into the shower water.

"Because I asked you to," I say with a wink, and he grins. "Good to know you're listening."

"Do I look like I've got enough brain cells to think about anything but you on the ride home?" he asks.

I pause for a beat, then burst out laughing and

cover my mouth as he steps into the shower and quickly rinses the grime off himself.

"You need to stop making people think you're a dumbass, we've been over this!" I tease when I get a hold of myself, bumping my hips to him as soon as he's in the shower. "People are going to believe it eventually."

"I've always thought it was for the better that way," he says, his voice growing less playful and more sensual as it lowers to a husky growl. "Stay quiet, let people think what they want, and let my hands do the talking."

"I've been waiting to talk with you all day," I say as a smile spreads across my face, and Big Daddy grins as he grips my hips and presses a kiss to my lips.

I feel his tongue dive into me as he walks me back to the cool tile wall of the shower, where my wet black hair gets pressed to the tile while his thick lips brush over my cheek and kiss me over and over. His teeth make their way down to my neck, and he opens his mouth wider to bite me gently as he towers over me.

I'm totally dwarfed by him, as always. My hands start to slide up his hips dand feel his abs, and every time I count them, my hands nearly shake at how hard they are. The simple, primal power this man can wield in his body never ceases to amaze me.

His greedy hands palm my breasts, and I let my head fall back as I wallow in the sensation he's warming up in me, teasing out my every little nerve and caressing me into a frenzy of feeling that I've already been sensitive to. "I've been thinking about you the whole time you've been gone," I confess into his ear as his nose brushes past some of my thick, wet hair and tickles my neck.

"I won't be able to focus on anything for a while," he says, slowly taking a step back and reaching out of the shower for something on the sink nearby. I see him open the switchblade and smile at me menacingly, and I feel my body warming sinfully as I lick my lips. "Maybe I should kidnap you again and bring you with me on the long rides coming up."

"I don't think I'd mind that," I say, shivering as he corners me in the shower and wraps an arm around my waist.

Ever so carefully, so practiced as he always was, he traces the edge of the blade along the most sensitive parts of my neck and down between my collarbone as I watched the gleaming steel and felt my skin electrify. His cock slid against my pussy and ground against me, sending a warm, glowing shiver through my body.

"Are you going to do as I say?" he growls in a low, ominous tone that makes me swallow.

"Anything," I breathe, my body quivering.

"Call me Daddy," he demands with a malicious grin.

"Fuck you," I breathe.

"You'll do that too, little girl," he growls, making my body melt as he squeezes me tight and holds the blade to my throat.

I take a deep breath, closing my eyes and feeling the glowing pleasure radiating from that spot where his hardened spear-shaft is pressed against my clit. While he speaks, he grinds up and down, and I feel a warm rush of bliss that comes with the "threat."

"Yes, Daddy," I finally say, feeling a satisfied pulse from his shaft at that.

"Good girl," he growls, taking the knife away from my throat, closing the blade, and tossing it to the rug outside before shutting the door. "Now open up for Daddy."

I feel him hoist me off my feet and pin me against the wall, and I bring my hands around to the back of his neck instinctively to hold myself up just before I feel him slide into me. He takes no time, and he doesn't even need to--I'm already slick and wet, and I have been since I stepped into the shower and knew I'd be here when he arrived.

"Fuck, *fuck!*" I squeak as that thick, vein-ribbed girth slides further into my pussy and fills me up so completely that I feel heat blossom from within and send me floating through a dream in a matter of moments.

Big Daddy wastes no time in rutting into me. I know this look in his eye, he has a primal need he has to work out. I feel that bulging purple crown pushing deep into me, pulsing and throbbing every inch that he drives in me. I can feel our juices mixing as he ruts further into me, and I drag my fingernails across the back of his neck as I grasp for stability.

I wrap my legs around his waist at the ankles. He's braced himself, and that iron body isn't going anywhere. His pelvis ruts freely into me as those heavy, virile balls swing with such a beautiful promise swelling up inside them. All I can think about him bursting inside me, like the same ferocious drive that pushes him to fuck me this way is infectious. It's like a pheromone in the air through that masculine scent the water tries to wash away, and I bask in it lavishly as I feel the first orgasm sneak up on me.

My toes clench, and I let out a gasping cry as I feel tension clench in my lower abdomen and spread out like rays of the sun, warming my body in a way the hot water never could. I pant shamelessly for him as he gropes me and kisses me, never letting me have a second to myself as I welcome him into me with hard, fast thrusts.

He groans, and the husky grunting I can hear from his throat is getting more raspy and less regular. I feel his precome spill into me, and I could almost laugh, I feel so overwhelmingly complete. The bulging crown pulses, and my husband presses a heartfelt kiss to my lips as he comes inside me, no condom, nothing but raw skin against skin and my honey mixing with his with every last thrust. He bucks wild into me as my own orgasm wracks my body so hard that I bite his lip, and he growls in dark laughter as he keeps rutting into me to put every last drop of that thick seed between my legs.

Those kinds of thoughts don't come through my mind that often--at least, they didn't until him.

"I love you," I breathe as it comes to an end, even though he's still hard as a rock inside me. "I love you so fucking much. *Daddy*," I add, not wanting to sound like *too* much of a sap, but he most definitely gets the message as his face practically glows in love.

"Daddy loves you too," he teases, nipping at my neck again before slowly sliding out of me. He holds me, kissing me tenderly, and he caresses my breasts as we lean against the shower together.

Just me and my kidnapper, looking ahead to a future we can be proud of as husband and wife.

The orgasm wells up inside me as I feel Big Daddy's tongue lavishing my clit with attention, his hands spreading over my belly as I dig my fingers into the thick winter bedsheets and let out a sharp gasp. My whole body convulses as I feel heat blossoming from my soaking-wet pussy. Big Daddy licks my lips clean as I wrap my legs around the back of his neck and try to press him harder against me.

He laughs sloppily into my pussy as my helpless body twitches and gets goosebumps. He knows exactly what keeps me going and how to ease me down from an orgasm, and my melted body goes limp at last as I feel a sweet shiver run up me.

"I love winter," I sigh as my bare legs slide off him while he stands up.

"Because there's nothing to do up here but stay

indoors and fuck between rides?" he growls, face glistening in the bedroom light around that bright white grin. "Yeah, it's growing on me, too. It's not even the coldest it's gonna get, either."

"We'll just have to get warmer," I say, pushing myself up into the sheets and covering myself as the chill in the room starts to reach me again. I wrap the blankets around me until I'm a lump swaddled in black cloth with a face poking out, watching Big Daddy's nude body clean himself off.

He wipes his face off with a towel, then does the same for the thick, satisfied cock hanging between his legs. I can still taste him on my lips, and it gives me the same rush it did the first time I gave him oral.

"What says 'biker Christmas party' in my wardrobe?" he grunts with a raised eyebrow as he opens the closet and steps aside.

"I was about to ask you the same question," I say.

"I think you're good like that," he says after a quick glance up and down my bed-nugget form. He strides over to my face peep-hole and leans in to kiss me, and I feel my face turn a faint shade of pink.

"Just roll me through the snow," I say. "Put goggles on me and strap me to your back on the way to the party. If anyone asks questions, tell them I'm just a cask of bootleg cider."

He snorts a laugh. "Save that idea for the wedding. It might make your mom throw less of a fit over the whole idea."

"You know Mom loves you," I say, laughing softly.

"No, you two have gotten a hell of a lot closer, I think there's a lot you could get away with that wouldn't bother her," he says jokingly, as if we aren't grown adults.

He's right, too. My brother was never very close to the family, so I think my mom was almost expecting it when she got the news that he had passed. I told her it had just been a gang incident. She doesn't need to know more details, much less that I was there for it. She had been preparing for that news for a lot longer than I realized, and that took some of the sting out.

Still, Pam had lost her son, and I'd lost a brother. It's been kind of a wakeup call for both of us. I've been making a point to meet up with my mom regularly even after she's gotten better, and she's been taking steps to improve her life that I never thought I'd see her do. She's even trying to quit smoking.

"Alright, Christmas fashion. For you, I'm thinking what you had picked out for underwear is my only input for the outfit," he says, holding up the lacey lingerie we picked up on our last trip to Denver before the snow started falling.

"That's a given," I say, nodding and slowly unraveling my bundle to step out toward the closet and start slipping into the expensive black fabric he bought for me. "But I'm thinking…"

I quickly slip into a thick pair of leggings, a large black wool sweater that hangs low, and a thick gray scarf that I can easily bundle around me so snugly I'll be downright hot in my clothing shell, and it just so happens to go well with my black beanie.

"You're wearing the turtleneck," I inform him.

"I knew you'd say that," my husband says with a warm smile. "Dick."

"It's a good turtleneck, you're the dick!" I say, correctly, while he pinches my ass as soon as the underwear is on me. "Wear it. And no underwear, if I'm wearing the lace. That's the deal," I say with a smirk and a wink."

"That's a bargain," he says with a chuckle.

We get dressed up and pick up the handful of presents we have for our friends and family--which have become one and the same since I've moved to Pine Haven. This little community has done nothing but grow in the few months that I've been here, and considering how small and underserved it is, I've had no trouble finding work as a caretaker.

Of course, I barely need to. Big Daddy's income and the collective the MC works with has me more than taken care of. There wasn't even a period where they kept me at arm's length. The second the smoke cleared and I asked Big Daddy what he thought about me moving to Pine Haven, the whole MC was ready to greet me with open arms.

The outside of the Heartbreaker MC is wrapped

to a fire hazard level in multicolored lights that twinkle in the darkness as Big Daddy's bike comes to a stop in the row of others that are lined up outside. There's a small army of bikes around by now, and I swear it gets bigger every time I see it.

I slip my arm into Big Daddy's as we trudge through the snowy dirt of the parking lot while I breathe in the crisp winter air and smell the aroma of food coming from the clubhouse. "Oh my god, tell me they've got the barbecue wings in for tonight," I say as my stomach growls.

"Yes ma'am we do," Big Daddy says with a downright ominous hunger. "And I take it that means we're both about to make 'em run out early."

"That's what I'm thinking, it's the holidays," I say with a smirk as we head inside.

Warmth and joy greets me the second we step in, and I beam around at the sights and sounds that all seem to glow just inside. The walls are all covered with different colors of lights, and on the far wall, Kate and Lauren have painstakingly arranged red lights against white that spell out the Heartbreaker name and emblem.

The tables are absolutely full of bikers and prospects, many of them in Santa hats (and a few ironic Satan horns, because Bones is an asshole), all of them in their kuttes. I'm proud to stand next to a turtlenecked Big Daddy as he dominates the room with his presence, and we make the rounds of greeting everyone. The numbers have swelled. A community elderly outreach program I've helped organize has really warmed the town up to the Heartbreakers, and we're seeing more people come looking to become prospects than ever.

Kate is about to burst and due at any moment. We've been taking bets on whether her baby will have a holiday birthday or not. My bet is that it'll be a New Year's baby, but I have a feeling Kate thinks it'll be sooner than that. Breaker hovers around her lovingly, and the rest of the club looks off to the two of them as they lead the way to starting families in the MC. The culture is starting to change, too. When I showed up, I was worried about this being a grungy frat house of dudes with too much testosterone and anger issues. To be fair, I did marry one of those, but mine turns his anger in the right direction.

This is more than that. It's a community that works together--a family.

Bones and Lauren are helping out in the kitchen together, so I don't see much of them for the evening, but I see the fruits of their labor coming out while Big Daddy takes on Ironside in darts as we start to pass around the bourbon egg nog. Cuts of turkey dark meat so flavorfully seasoned that I can barely believe it's turkey seem to be the crowd favorite. I've got my eye on the chalkboard menu, and the sweet potato casserole is making my stomach growl.

The kitchen is still a new addition to the clubhouse, but it's taken no time to get popular. These are still bikers, of course, which is probably why the next most popular menu items coming out of the kitchen are thick burgers stuffed with shredded barbecue pork as well as chicken and waffle platters that pair all too well with the drinks.

Everyone's about to gain five pounds or so tonight, myself included. It's going to be great.

Justine is passing around the egg nog, and I've just accepted a *healthy* glass of it when Lauren emerges from the kitchen, waving to everyone as Kate swoops by to give her a hug. "We miss you! Are you sure one of us can't tag-team with you and give you a break? Skid could use some kitchen experience, and you need some bourbon in you."

"Agreed," Big Daddy and I say at the same time before I drain a huge gulp of mine, and the others laugh as Lauren blushes and holds up a hand.

"No nog for me, actually," she says, laughing softly.

"You can take some back to the kitchen," Justine says, smiling and swaying the egg nog temptingly. "I'll pour you a Big Girl Glass."

"Actually, I kind of slipped out because I have an announcement I thought it would be better to make before we start going ham on some good-ass food and drinks," she says with a grin, and the others nearby turn to attention as Breaker comes to hug Kate and I raise my eyebrows.

Bones comes out of the kitchens too, looking proud, and my mouth falls open with a smile before she can even start talking.

"I'm two months pregnant," Lauren says, looking up at Bones and beaming lovingly as the rest of us burst into applause, and I'm the first to swoop in and hug her tight after she breaks away from Bones before the rest of us start passing her around with adoration.

"We're going to have a pack of kids following the bikes around by the end of next year at this rate," Ironside says with a laugh, and Justine blushes as she hugs Lauren.

"Can't think of a better way to start off a Christmas feast," Breaker says, smiling around at the Heartbreakers as we stand together in a room full of loving faces--a family that's only going to grow larger. "And I can't think of a better family to spend it with. Merry Christmas, you crusty fucks!"

There's a roar of approval from the club that I join in on, already feeling the buzz of the bourbon in me as Big Daddy hugs me tight, proud of me as I am to be at his side.

Warmer than ever--for the rest of our lives.

Trafficked

Stealing Her

The Assassin's Heart

Killing For Her

Abducted

KILLERS:

Hunter's Baby

I Hired A Hitman

STEPBROTHERS:

Ruthless

Criminal

GLITZ & GRIT:

Betting on Love

Vegas Boss

Rock Hard Bodyguard

Innocence For Sale: Jane

Redeeming Viktor

SEXY SEALs

Sweetheart for the SEAL

Sights on the SEAL

Romance:

Falling for her Boss (Novella)

Most Wanted: Lilly (Novella)

Bound as the World Burns (SFF)

<u>**Erotic Thriller:**</u>

THE DANGEROUS MEN SERIES:

The Narrow Path

Strayed from the Path

Path to Ruin

ABOUT THE AUTHOR

Alexis Abbott is a Wall Street Journal & USA Today bestselling author who writes about bad boys protecting their girls! Pick up her books today if you can't resist a bad boy who is a good man, and find yourself transported with super steamy sex, gritty suspense, and lots of romance.

She lives in beautiful St. John's, NL, Canada with her amazing husband.

facebook.com/abbottauthor

twitter.com/abbottauthor

instagram.com/alexisabbottauthor

bookbub.com/authors/alexis-abbott

pinterest.com/badboyromance

youtube.com/AlexisAbbott

ACKNOWLEDGMENTS

Thank you to my amazing Patrons. I'm constantly humbled and grateful for your support.

Ramona Cabrera
Melissa Hedrick
Virginia Swanson
Dawn Daughenbaugh
Don Doss
Stacie Currie

If you'd like to join them — and get my ebooks or paperbacks — you can find me here on Patreon.
https://www.patreon.com/alexisabbott